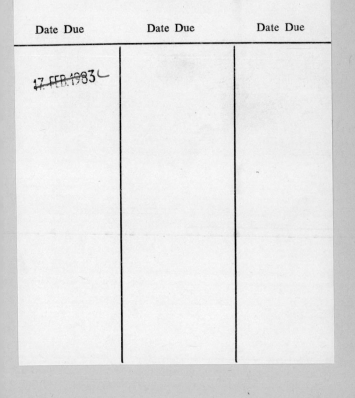

ST. MARY'S COLLEGE OF EDUCATION

LIBRARY

Date Due	Date Due	Date Due
17 FEB 1983		

Desire

and other stories

JAMES STEPHENS

Selected and introduced by
Augustine Martin

poolbeg press

First published 1980 by
Poolbeg Press Ltd.,
Knocksedan House,
Swords, Co. Dublin, Ireland.

© Iris Wise, The Estate of James Stephens 1981.

Cover picture by kind permission of The National Gallery
of Ireland.

Book and cover designed by Steven Hope.

Printed by Cahill Printers Limited,
East Wall Road, Dublin 3.

Contents

This book is one of a series devoted to the modern Irish short story. Ireland's contribution to the short story is world famous, but much of the best work both of the acknowledged masters and of the new hands is either out of print or has never been published in book form. The aim of this series is to make that work generally available.

Introduction

James Stephens was probably born in Dublin on February 2, 1882, within hours of James Joyce. The few facts that have been established about his early years suggest hardship and deprivation: he entered the Meath Protestant Industrial School for Boys at the age of four and remained there for ten years. Between the years 1896 and 1912 he worked as a solicitor's clerk in Dublin. By that time he had not only established himself as a foremost Irish writer but had published significantly in a variety of *genres*. His first collection of poems, *Insurrections*, had appeared in 1909; his novel, *The Charwoman's Daughter*, his prose fantasy, *The Crock of Gold,* and his second poetry volume, *The Hill of Vision*, had all appeared in 1912; his play, *Julia Elizabeth,* had been produced in 1911 by the Theatre of Ireland.

The celebrity of his two major prose fictions tended to obscure his achievement in the short story, though it was his promise in the shorter form that enabled him to move to Paris for a year in 1913 and devote himself to a literary career.

It was in that year that a London magazine, *The Nation*, offered him a commission to write a series of stories for publication in its pages. He had been publishing sketches in Arthur Griffith's newspaper, *Sinn Fein*, since 1907, and was engaged in assembling them into the collection *Here Are Ladies* which came out with the additional, and much finer, *Nation* stories in October of 1913. His only other collection, *Etched in Moonlight*, appeared in 1928, though in the intervening years he experimented continually with the short story form.

A great deal has been made of the colourful coincidences between the careers of Stephens and Joyce — born at the same time in the same city, the former's second name being the christian name of Joyce's hero and so on. Both writers in their later years cherished these correspondances and it is a matter of record that Joyce asked Stephens to finish *Finnegans Wake* should he die before its completion. But the parallels between their careers as short story writers are even more intriguing, and are of genuine significance in the development of the form within the Irish tradition.

Both writers began in the first years of the century by publishing sketches, which they afterwards reworked, in Dublin newspapers. Each brought out his first volume while abroad, sending on stories of increasing weight and excellence after the first version of the book had been submitted to its publisher. Both concentrated on the Dublin middle and lower middle classes as their main fictional material. *Here Are Ladies* and *Dubliners* (1914) came out within months of each other.

The Irish short story at that time was in its infancy. George Moore's seminal work, *The Untilled Field* (1903), ante-dated Stephens's volume by an exact decade and nothing significant had been published in the interim. Stephens therefore shared the first thrust of the form with Moore and Joyce. The second phase was to begin with Daniel Corkery's *A Munster Twilight* which came out, significantly, in 1916 and which was so quickly to be followed by the mature work of Seumas O'Kelly, and that of O'Flaherty, O'Connor and O'Faolain.

This is not to suggest that Joyce was an early admirer of Stephens's work. If we are to believe Stephens's droll account of their first meeting it is a miracle that they ever became friends. The incident is described in one of the poet's celebrated radio broadcasts published by Lloyd Frankenberg in *James Seamus and Jacques:*

> He turned his chin and his specs at me, and away down at me, and confided the secret to me that he had read my two books; that, grammatically, I did not know the difference between a semi-colon and a colon: that my knowledge of Irish life was non-Catholic and, so, non-existent, and that I should give up writing and take to a good job like shoe-shining as a more promising profession.
>
> I confided back to him that I had never read a word of his, and that, if Heaven preserved to me my protective wits, I never would read a word of his, unless I was asked to destructively review it.

Indeed, if it had not been for the protective encouragment of A.E., Stephens might well have been crushed by the disapprobation of his more established contemporaries. Shaw returned some of the younger poet's manuscripts with the remark that he 'could not be bothered with such illiterate stuff.' George Moore could see initially 'little more than harsh versification, and crude courage in the choice of subjects.' Stephens, together with F.R. Higgins, was among the 'bad poets' derided by Yeats in his famous epigram which ends: 'But was there ever dog that praised his fleas?' Yet all of them revised their views of Stephens's accomplishment and most of them became his personal friends.

The Stephens short story is a startlingly original conception, owing very little to his predecessors in the trade, and making, as far as I can judge, no distinctive impact on his Irish successors. In the field of the novel, especially of the prose fantasy, his influence has been substantial: Eimar O'Duffy, Flann O'Brien, Austin Clarke, Mervyn Wall, Bryan Mac Mahon and Joyce himself cannot have escaped his example in adapting the Celtic hero to comic or satiric ends; in exploiting the mock heroic possibilities of Gaelic prose patterns; or in blending the mythic and the fabulous with the quotidian and realistic. In these distinctively Irish fictional developments *The Demi-Gods* must be acknowledged a seminal work. But from the outset the short story in Stephens's hands seems to have pursued a consistent yet experimental destiny of its own.

Here Are Ladies, as I have pointed out in my book on the writer, is conceived — and again the parallel with *Dubliners* is instructive — as an integrated work rather than as a mere collection of separate stories. It combines poems, cameos and formal short stories in triadic patterns to build a sort of contrapuntal comedy of the sexual life. If Stephens had not been working against the pressure of time and economic necessity this pattern might have been wrought into something unique and marvellous. As it happened, his publisher kept demanding more material to make up bulk and the author was forced to destroy his symmetries by adding a number of slight and irrelevant sketches, and that long series of monologues, 'There is a Tavern in the Town', which had already appeared as humorous journalism in *Sinn Fein*. The symmetrical pattern, while it lasted — for 250 pages — can be represented like this:

POEM	TRIAD OF CAMEOS	STORY
Women	*Three Heavy Husbands*	*A Glass of Beer*
One and One	*Three Women Who Wept*	*The Triangle*
The Daisies	*Three Angry People*	*The Threepenny Piece*
Brigid	*Three Young Wives*	*The Horses*
Mistress Quiet Eyes	*Three Lovers Who Lost*	*The Blind Man*

As this book is a selection of Stephens's best stories it was necessary to disturb this pattern by discarding the poems and a number of the weaker camoes together with the dead wood that encumbers the latter section of the book. But it is useful to know that the scheme existed, because the poem in each case introduced a love-theme, the triad developed it in three variations, and the story brought it to a more or less serious

9

resolution. The over-riding concern was Stephens's obsessive sense of the war between the sexes, a theme which could issue in such exquisite humour and lyricism as the third section of *Three Heavy Husbands* or in the nightmare misogyny of *The Glass of Beer* or *The Blind Man*. Anyone who still holds the picture of Stephens as the whimsical lyricist, Ireland's answer to Kenneth Milne, has only to read these two stories to have his vision revised. There is nothing in the Irish short story before or since so mordant and scarifying.

That is unless one discounts the stories from his next volume, *Etched in Moonlight*, only one of which, *The Boss*, is omitted from the present collection. Here, in the opening story, a deceptively casual domestic anecdote develops in sleep to a nightmare of emotional isolation and despair. In the title story dream is again deployed to explore the psychology of sexual jealousy and its corrosive effects on the psyche. The power of the prose in this remarkable fable, its nuances of colour and atmosphere, its ability to create a world of archetypal obsession, is comparable with that of James in *The Turn of the Screw* or Poe in *The Pit and the Pendulum*. By a strange irony the same stylistic resource distils, in perhaps his greatest story, *Hunger*, a drama of archetypal desperation from the sufferings of a Dublin working class family who perish at the hands of man's oldest and most commonplace enemy. This story was published in 1918 as a separate booklet under the pseudonym 'James Esse'. We have his word that 'The Story is a true one, and would have killed me but that I got it out of my system this way.' The intensity

10

of the social concern embodied in *Hunger* reminds us of Stephens's vehement anti-clerical letter from Paris to *The Irish Worker* in 1913 written in solidarity with Larkin's workers during the great Lock-Out and entitled *Get off that Fence*. It is a theme that animates many of his earliest lyrics in *Insurrections,* re-emerges in the interpolated tales of *The Crock of Gold* and receives vivid and extended treatment in the story of Billy the Music in *The Demi-Gods.* The last piece in the present selection, *A Rhinosceros, Some Ladies, and a Horse*, is included with some reluctance. It has done Stephens's reputation a great deal of disservice being almost invariably chosen to represent him in short story anthologies, even though it was not written as a short story but as the first chapter of an autobiography which he abandoned in 1946. It shows the writer at his most whimsical, and has helped to reinforce the impression of Stephens as the untroubled fantasist which is the image so many readers have taken from a superficial reading of that serious and subversive book, *The Crock of Gold*. But the fragment is genuinely hilarious. It makes a suitable ending for a selection which begins cheerfully but moves on through so many dark reaches of the human predicament in the great central stories. And it does, after all, present that side of Stephens that most of his readers persist in loving best.

AUGUSTINE MARTIN

Three Heavy Husbands

I

He had a high nose. He looked at one over the collar, so to speak. His regard was very assured, and his speech was that short bundle of monosyllables which the subaltern throws at the orderly. He had never been questioned, and, the precedent being absent, he had never questioned himself. Why should he? We live by question and answer, but we do not know the reply to anything until a puzzled comrade bothers us and initiates that divine curiosity which both humbles and uplifts us.

He wanted all things for himself. What he owned he wished to own completely. He would give anything away with the largest generosity, but he would share with no one.

'Whatever is mine,' said he, 'must be entirely mine. If it is alive I claim its duty to the last respiration of its breath, and if it is dead I cannot permit a mortgage on it. Have you a claim on anything belonging to me? then you may have it entirely, I must have all of it or none.'

He was a stockbroker, and, by the methods peculiar to that mysterious profession, he had captured a sufficiency of money to enable him regard the future with calmness and his fellow-creatures with condescension—perhaps the happiest state to which a certain humanity can attain.

So far matters were in order. There remained nothing to round his life into the complete, harmonious circle except a wife; but as a stated income has the choice of a large supply, he shortly discovered a lady whose qualifications were such as would ornament any, however exalted, position. She was sound in wind and limb. She spoke grammar with the utmost precision, and she could play the piano with such skill that it was difficult to explain why she played it badly.

This also was satisfactory, and if the world had been made of machinery he would have had the fee-simple of happiness. But to both happiness and misery there follows the inevitable second act, and beyond that, and to infinity, action and interaction, involution and evolution, forging change for ever. Thus he failed to take into consideration that the lady was alive, that she had a head on her shoulders which was native to her body, and that she could not be aggregated as chattel property for any longer period than she agreed to.

After their marriage he discovered that she had dislikes which did not always coincide with his, and appreciations which set his teeth on edge. A wife in the house is a critic on the hearth—this truth was daily and unpleasantly impressed upon him: but, of course, every man knows that every woman is a fool, and a tolerant smile is the only recognition we allow to their whims. God made them as they are—we grin and bear it.

His wife found that the gospel of her husband was this—Love me to the exclusion of all human creatures. Believe in me even when I am in the wrong. Women should be seen and not heard. When you want excitement make a fuss of your husband. But while he entirely forgot that his wife had been bought and paid for, she did not forget it: indeed, she could not help remembering it. A wrong had been done her not to be obscured even by economics, the great obscurer. She had been won and not wooed. (The very beasts have their privileges!) She had been defrauded of how many teasing and provoking prerogatives, aloofnesses, and surrenders, and her body, if not her mind, resented and remembered it.

There are times when calmness is not recognized as a virtue. Of course, he had wooed her in a way. He took her to the opera, he gave her jewels, he went to church with her twice every Sunday, and once a month he knelt beside her in more profound reverences: sometimes he petted her, always he was polite.

But he had not told her that her eyes were the most wonderful and inspiring orbs into which a tired man could look. He never said that there would not be much to choose between good and evil if he lost her. He never said that one touch of her lips would electrify a paralytic into an acrobat. He never swore that he would commit suicide and dive to deep perdition if she threw him over—none of these things. It is possible that she did not wish him to say or do

15

such extravagances, but he had not played the game, and, knowing that something was badly wrong, she nursed a grievance, that horrid fosterling.

He was fiercely jealous, not of his love, but of his property, and while he was delighted to observe that other men approved of his taste, he could not bear that his wife should admire these outsiders. This was his attitude to her: Give me your admirations, all of them, every note of exclamation of which you are mistress, every jot and tittle of your thoughts must be mine, for, lacking these, I have nothing. I am good to you. I have interposed between you and the buffets of existence. I temper all winds to the bloom of your cheek. Do you your part, and so we will be happy.

There was a clerk in his office, a black-haired, slim, frowning young man, who could talk like a cascade for ten minutes and be silent for a month: he was a very angry young man, with many hatreds and many ambitions. His employer prized him as a reliable and capable worker, liked his manners, and paid him thirty-five shillings per week—outside of these matters the young man abode no more in his remembrance than did the flower on the heath or the bird on the tree.

It happened one day that the employer fell sick of influenza and was confined to his bed. This clerk, by order, waited on him to see to his correspondence; for, no matter who sneezes, work must be attended to.

The young man stayed in the house for a week, and during his sojourn there he met the lady. She fair, young, brooding! he also young, silent, and angry! After the first look had passed between them, there was little more to be said. They came together as though they had been magnetised. Love or passion, by whatever name it is called, was born abruptly. There is a force in human relations drawing too imperatively for denial; defying self-interest, and dragging at all anchors of duty and religion. Is it in man only the satisfaction of self? Egotism standing like a mountain, and demanding, 'Give me yourself or I will kill myself.' And women! is their love the degradation of self, the surrender and very abasement of lowliness? or is it also egotism set on a pinnacle, so careless and self-assured as to be fearful of nothing? In their eyes the third person, a shadow already, counted as less than a shadow. He was a name with no significance, a something without a locality. His certain and particular income per annum was a thing to laugh at. . .there was a hot, a swift voice speaking—'I love you,' it said, 'I love you': he would batter his way into heaven, he would tear delight from whatever delight might be— or else, and this was harder, a trembling man pleading, 'Aid me or I perish,' and it is woman's instinct not to let a man perish. 'If I help you, I hurt myself,' she sighed; and, 'Hurt yourself, then,' sighed the man; 'would you have me perish. . .?'

So the owner by purchase smiled—

'You are mine,' said he, 'altogether mine, no one else has a lien upon you. When the weather is fine I will take you for drives in the sunshine. In the nights we will go to the opera, hearkening together to the tenor telling his sweet romanza, and when the wintry rain beats on the windows you will play the piano for me, and so we will be happy.'

When he was quite recovered he went back to his office, and found that one of his clerks had not arrived—this angered him; when he returned home again in the evening, he found that his wife was not there. So things go.

II

He was one of those who shy at the tête-à-tête life which, for a long time, matrimony demands. As his wedding-day approached he grew fearful of the prolonged conversation which would stretch from the day of marriage, down the interminable vistas, to his death, and, more and more, he became doubtful of his ability to cope with, or his endurance to withstand, the extraordinary debate called marriage.

He was naturally a silent man. He did not dislike conversation if it was kept within decent limits: indeed, he responded to it contentedly enough, but when he had spoken or been addressed for more than an hour he became, first, impatient, then bored, and, finally, sulky or ill-mannered. 'With men,' said he, 'one can talk or be silent as one wishes, for between them there is a community of understanding which turns the occasional silence into a pregnant and fruitful interlude wherein a thought may keep itself warm until it is wanted: but with a woman!—he could not pursue that speculation further, for his acquaintance with the sex was limited.

In every other respect his bride was a happiness. Her good looks soothed and pleased him. The touch of her hand gave him an extraordinary pleasure which concealed within it a yet more extraordinary excitement. Her voice, as a mere sound, enchanted him. It rippled and flowed, deepened and tinkled. It cooed and sang to him at times like the soft ring-dove calling to its mate, and, at times again, it gurgled and piped like a thrush happy in the sunlight. The infinite variation of her tone astonished and delighted him, and if it could have remained something as dexterous and impersonal as a wind he would have been content to listen to it for ever—but, could he give her pipe for pipe? Would the rich gurgle or the soft coo sound at last as a horrid iteration, a mere clamour to which he must not only give an obedient heed, but must even answer from a head wherein silence had so peacefully brooded?

His mind was severe, his utterance staccato, and he had no knowledge of those conversational arts whereby nouns and verbs are amazingly transfigured into a gracious frolic or an intellectual pleasure. To snatch the chatter from its holder, toss and keep it playing in the air until another snatched it from him; to pluck a theory hot from the stating, and expand it until it was as iridescent and, perhaps, as thin as a soap-bubble; to light up and vivify a weighty conversation until the majestic thing sparkled and glanced like a jewel,—these things he could not do, and he knew it. Many a time he had sat, amazed as at an exhibition of acrobatics, while around him the chatter burst and sang and shone. He had tried to bear his part, but had never been able to edge more than one word into that tossing cataract, and so he fell to the habit of listening instead of speaking.

With some reservations, he enjoyed listening, but particularly he enjoyed listening to his own thoughts as they trod slowly, but very certainly, to foregone conclusions. Into the silent arena of his mind no impertinent chatterer could burst with a mouthful of puns or ridicule, or a reminiscence caught on the wing and hurled apropos to the very centre of discussion. His own means of conveying or gathering information was that whereby one person asked a question and another person answered it, and, if the subject proved deeper than the assembled profundity, then one pulled out the proper volume of an encyclopaedia, and the pearl was elicited as with a pin.

Meanwhile, his perturbation was real. There are people to whom we need not talk—let them pass: we overlook or smile distantly at the wretches, retaining our reputation abroad and our self-respect in its sanctuary: but there are others with whom we may not be silent, and into this latter category a wife enters with assured emphasis. He foresaw endless opportunities for that familiar discussion to which he was a stranger. There were breakfast-tables, dinner-tables, tea-tables, and, between these, there might be introduced those preposterous other tables which women invent for no purpose unless it be that of making talk. His own breakfast, dinner, and tea tables had been solitary ones, whereat he lounged with a newspaper propped against a lamp, or a book resting one end against the sugar-bowl and the other against his plate. This quietude would be ravaged from him for ever, and that tumult nothing could exorcise or impede. Further than these, he foresaw an interminable drawing-room, long walks together, and other, even more confidential and particular, sequestrations.

After one has married a lady, what does one say

to her? He could not conceive any one saying anything beyond 'Good-morning.' Then the other aspect arrested him, 'What does a women find to say to a man?' Perhaps safety lay in this direction, for they were reputed noteable and tireless speakers to whom replies are not pressingly necessary. He looked upon his sweetheart as from a distance, and tried to reconstruct her recent conversations. He was amazed at the little he could remember. 'I, I, I; we, we, we; this shop, that shop; Aunt Elsa, and chocolates.' She had mentioned all these things on the previous day, but she did not seem to have said anything memorable about them, and, so far as he could recollect, he had said nothing in reply but 'Oh yes' and 'To be sure!' Could he sustain a lifetime of small-talk on these meagre responses? He saw in vision his most miserable tea-table—a timid husband and a mad wife glaring down their noses at plates. The picture leaped at him as from a cinematograph and appalled him. . .After a time they would not even dare to look at each other. Hatred would crouch behind these figures, waiting for its chain to be loosed!

So he came to the knowledge that he, so soon to be a husband, had been specially fashioned by nature to be a bachelor. For him safety lay in solitude: others, less rigorously planned, might safely venture into the haphazard, gregarious state of wedlock, but he not only could not, but must not, do so, and he meditated an appeal to his bride to release him from the contract. Several times the meditation almost became audible, but always, just as he toppled on the surge of speech, the dear lady loosed a torrent of irrelevancies which swirled him from all anchorage, and left him at the last stranded so distantly from his thought that he did not know how to find his way back to it.

It would be too brutally direct to shatter information about silk at one shilling the yard with a prayer for matrimonial freedom. The girl would be shocked—he could see her—she would stare at him, and suddenly grow red in the face and stammer; and he would be forced to trail through a lengthy, precise explanation of this matter which was not at all precise to himself. Furthermore, certain obscure emotions rendered him unwilling to be sundered from this girl. There was the touch of her hand; more, the touch of her lips given bravely and with ready modesty—a contact not lightly to be relinquished. He did not believe he could ever weary of looking at her eyes: they were grey, widely open, and of a kindness such as he could not disbelieve in; a radiant cordiality, a soft, limpid goodwill; believing and trustful eyes which held no guile when they looked at him: there were her movements, her swiftness, spaciousness, her buoyant certainty: one remembered her hair, her hands, the way she wore a frock, and a strange, seductive something about the look of her shoe.

The thing was not possible! It is the last and darkest insult to tell the woman who loves you that you do not wish to marry her. Her indignant curiosity may be appeased only by the excuse that you like some other woman better, and although she may hate the explanation she will understand it—but no less legitimate excuse than this may pass sunderingly between a man and a woman.

It lay, therefore, that he must amend his own

hand, and, accordingly, for the purpose of marital intercourse, he began a sad inquiry into the nature of things. The world was so full of things: clouds and winds and sewing machines, kings and brigands, hats and heads, flower-pots, jam, and public-houses —surely one could find a little to chat about at any moment if one were not ambitiously particular. With inanimate objects one could speak of shape and colour and usefulness. Animate objects had, beside these, movements and aptitudes for eating and drinking, playing and quarrelling. Artistic things were well or badly executed, and were also capable of an inter-comparison which could not but be interesting and lengthy. These things could all be talked about. There were positive and negative qualities attaching to everything, and when the former was exhausted the latter could still be profitably mined — 'Order,' said he, 'subsists in everything, and even conversation must be subject to laws capable of ascertainment.'

He carefully, and under the terms of badinage, approached other men, inquiring how they bore themselves in the matrimonial dispute, and what were the subjects usually spoken of in the intimacies of family life. But from these people he received the smallest assistance. Some were ribald, some jocose, some so darkly explanatory that intelligence could not peer through the mist or could only divine that these hated their wives. One man held that all domestic matters should be left entirely to the wife and that talking was a domestic matter. Another said that the words 'yes, no, and why' would safeguard a man through any labyrinth, however tortuous. Another said that he always went out when the wife began to speak; and yet another suggested that the only possible basis for conversation was that of perpetual opposition, where an affirmation was always countered by a denial, and the proving of the case exercised both time and intelligence.

As he sat in the train beside his wife the silence which he so dreaded came upon them. Emptiness buzzed in his head. He sought diligently for something to speak about—the characteristics of objects! There were objects and to spare, but he could not say—'That window is square, it is made of glass,' or, 'the roof of this carriage is flat, it is made of wood.'

Suddenly his wife buried her face in her muff, and her shoulders were convulsed. . . .

Love and contrition possessed him on the instant. He eased his husky throat, and the dreaded, interminable conversation began—

'What are you crying for, my dear?' said he.

Her voice, smothered by the fur, replied—

'I am not crying, darling,' said she, 'I am only laughing.'

III

He got stiffly up from his seat before the fire.

'Be hanged,' said he, 'if I wait any longer for her. If she doesn't please to come in before this hour let her stop out,' He stared into the fire for a few moments—'Let her go to Jericho,' said he, and he tramped up to bed.

They had been married just six months, after, as he put it, the hardest courtship a man ever undertook. She was more like a piece of quicksilver than a girl. She was as uncertain as a spring wind, as flighty as a ball of thistledown—'Doesn't know her own mind for ten minutes together,' he groaned. 'Hasn't any mind at all,' he'd think an hour later. While, on the following day, it might be—'That woman is too deep, she is dodging all round me, she is sticking her finger in my eye. She treats me as if I wasn't there at one moment, and diddles me as if I was Tom Fool the next—I'll get out of it.'

He had got out of it three or four times—halted her against a wall, and, with a furious forefinger, wagged all her misdeeds in her face; then, rating her up, down and round, he had prepared to march away complacent and refreshed like Justice taking leave of a sinner, only to find that if the jade wept he could not go away.

'Dash it all,' said he, 'you can't leave a girl squatting down against a wall, with her head in her lap and she crying. Hang it,' said he, 'you feel as if there was water round your legs and you'll splash if you move.'

So he leavened justice with mercy, and, having dried her tears with his lips, he found himself in the same position as before, with a mad suspicion tattering through his brain that maybe he had been 'diddled' again.

But he married her, and to do that was a job also. She shied at matrimony. She shied at everything that looked plain or straight. She was like a young dog out for a walk: when she met a side-street she bolted down it and was instantly surrounded by adventure and misery, returning, like the recovered pup, thick with the mud of those excursions. There was a lust in her blood for side-streets, laneways and corners.

'Marriage!' said she, and she was woe-begone—
'Marriage will be for ever.'

'So will heaven,' he retorted comfortingly.

'So will—the other place,' said she, with a giggle,
and crushed him under the feeling that she envisag-
ed him as the devil of that particular Hades, instead
of as an unfortunate sinner plucked up by the heels
and soused into the stew-pan by his wife.

He addressed himself—

'When we are married,' said he, 'I'll keep a hand
on you, my lady, that you won't be able to wriggle
away from. If you are slippery, and faith you are,
why I'm tough, and so you'll find it.' 'Get rid of
your kinks before you marry,' said he. 'I've no use
for a wife with one eye on me, and it a dubious
one, and the other one squinting into a parlour two
streets off. You've got to settle down and quit tricks.
A wife has no one else to deceive but her husband,
that's all she can want tricks for, and there's not
going to be any in my house. Its all right for a pretty
girl to be a bit larky—'

'Am I really pretty?' said she, deeply interested,
and leaning forward with her hands clasping her
knees— 'Do you really and truly think I am pretty?
I met a man one time, he had a brown moustache
and blue eyes, outside a tailor's shop in George's
Street, with a public-house on one side, and he said
he thought I was very pretty: he told me what his
name was, but I forget it: maybe you know him:
he wears a tweed suit with a stripe and a soft hat
let me see, no, his name began with a T—'

'His name was Thief,' he roared, 'and that was his
profession too. Don't let me catch you talking with
a strange man, or you'll get hurt, and his brown

eyes will be mixed up with his blue moustache.'

So married they were, six months now, and the wits were nearly worried out of him in trying to keep pace with his wife's vagaries. Matrimony had not cured her love for side-streets, short cuts and chance acquaintances, and she was gradually making her husband travel at a similar tangent. When they started to go to church he would find, to his amazement, that they were in the Museum. If they journeyed with a Museum for an objective they were certain to pull up in the Botanic Gardens. A call on a friend usually turned into a visit to a theatre or a walk by the Dodder.

'Heart-scalded I am,' said he, 'with her hopping and trotting. She travels sideways like a crab, so she does. She has a squint in her walk. Her boots have a bias outwards. I'm getting bow-legged, so I am, slewing round corners after her. I'll have to put my foot down,' said he.

And now it was all finished. Here was twelve o'clock at night and an absent wife—a detestable combination. Twelve o'clock at night outside a house is an immoral hour, inside a house it is nonmoral, but respectable. There is nothing in the street at that time but dubiety. Who would be a husband listening through the tolling of midnight for a muffled footfall? And he had told her not to go: had given an order, formulated his imperative and inflexible will.

'Never mind! I'll stand by it,' said he, 'this is the last straw. One break and then freedom. Surgery is better than tinkering. Cut the knot and let who will try to join it then. One pang, and afterwards ease, fresh air, and freedom: fresh air! gulps of it, with the head back and an easy mind. I'm not the man to be fooled for ever—surgery! surgery!'

His wife had wished to see a friend that night and requested her husband to go with her—he refused.

'You're always traipsin' about,' said he.

She entreated.

He heaved an angry forehead at her, puckered an eye, toned a long No that wagged vibration behind it like an undocked tail.

She persisted, whereupon he loosed his thunder.

'You're not to step outside the house this night, ma'am,' said he; and to her angry 'I will go,' he barked, 'If you do go, don't come back here. I'll have a dutiful wife or I'll have none—stay in or stay out. I'm tired humouring your whimsies, let you humour mine now—'

Then a flame gathered on her face, it grew hot in her voice, flashed to a point in her eyes.

'I'm going out to-night,' said she loudly; 'are you coming with me?'

'I'm not,' said he.

'Then,' she snapped, 'I'll go by myself.'

'Wherever you go to-night you can stay,' he roared. 'Don't come back to this house.'

'I'm not mad enough to want to,' she replied. 'I wish I'd never seen your old house. I wish I'd never seen yourself. You are just as dull as your house is, and nearly as flat. It's a stupid, uninteresting, slow house, so it is, and you are a stupid, dissatisfied grump of a man, so you are. I'd sooner live in a cave with a hairy bear, so I would—' And out she ran.

Two minutes later he had heard the door bang, and then silence.

That was five hours ago, and during all these long

hours he had sat staring sourly into the fire, seeing goodness knows what burnt-up visions therein, waiting to hear a footfall, and an entreating voice at the key-hole; apologies and tears perhaps, and promises of amendment. Now it was after twelve o'clock, darkness everywhere and silence. Time and again a policeman's tramp or the hasty, light footfall of adventure went by. So he stood up at last, sour and vindictive.

'She would have her fling. She wouldn't give in. She doesn't care a tinker's curse what I say. . . Let her go to Jericho,' said he, and he tramped up to bed.

In his bedroom he did not trouble to get a light. He undressed in a bitterly savage mood and rolled into bed, only to jump out again in sudden terror, for there was someone in it. It was his wife. He lay down with a hazy, half-mad mind. Had he wronged her? Was she more amenable than he had fancied? She had not gone out at all—or, had she gone out, sneaked in again by the back-door and crept noiselessly to bed. . .?

He fell asleep at last on the tattered fringe of a debate—Had he wronged her? or had she diddled him again?

A Glass of Beer

It was now his custom to sit there. The world has its habits, why should a man not have his? The earth rolls out of light and into darkness as punctually as a business man goes to and from his office; the seasons come with the regularity of automata, and go as if they were pushed by an ejector; so, night after night, he strolled from the Place de l'Observatoire to the Pont St. Michel, and, on the return journey, sat down at the same Café, at the same table, if he could manage it, and ordered the same drink.

So regular had his attendance become that the waiter would suggest the order before it was spoken. He did not drink beer because he liked it, but only because it was not a difficult thing to ask for. Always he had been easily discouraged, and he distrusted his French almost as much as other people had reason to. The only time he had varied the order was to request 'un vin blanc gommée,' but on that occasion he had been served with a postage stamp for twenty-five centimes, and he still wondered when he remembered it.

He liked to think of his first French conversation. He wanted something to read in English, but was timid of asking for it. He walked past all the newspaper kiosks on the Boulevard, anxiously scanning the vendors inside—they were usually very stalwart, very competent females, who looked as though they had outgrown their sins but remembered them with pleasure. They had the dully-polished, slightly-battered look of a modern antique. The words 'M'sieu, Madame' rang from them as from bells. They were very alert, sitting, as it were, on tiptoe, and their eyes hit one as one approached. They were like spiders squatting in their little houses waiting for their daily flies.

He found one who looked jolly and harmless, sympathetic indeed, and to her, with a flourished hat, he approached. Said he, 'Donnez-moi, Madame, s'il vous plaît, le *Daily Mail*.' At the second repetition the good lady smiled at him, a smile compounded of benevolence and comprehension, and instantly, with a 'V'la M'sieu,' she handed him *The New York Herald*. They had saluted each other, and he marched down the road in delight, with his first purchase under his arm and his first foreign conversation accomplished.

At that time everything had delighted him—the wide, well-lighted Boulevard, the concierges knitting in their immense doorways, each looking like a replica of the other, each seeming sister to a kiosk-keeper or a cat. The exactly-courteous speech of the people and their not quite so rigorously courteous manners pleased him. He listened to the voluble men who went by, speaking in a haste so breathless that he marvelled how the prepositions and conjunctions stuck to their duty in so swirling an ocean of chatter. There was a big black dog with a mottled head who lay nightly on the pavement opposite the Square de l'Observatoire. At intervals he raised his lean skull from the ground and composed a low lament to an absent friend. His grief was respected. The folk who passed stepped sidewards for him, and he took no heed of their passage—a lonely, introspective dog to whom a caress or a bone were equally childish things: Let me alone, he seemed to say, I have my grief, and it is company enough. There was the very superior cat who sat on every window-ledge, winking at life. He (for in France all cats are masculine by order of philology) did not care a rap for man or dog, but he liked women and permitted them to observe him. There was the man who insinuated himself between the tables at the Café, holding out postcard-representations of the Pantheon, the Louvre, Notre Dame, and other places. From beneath these cards his dexterous little finger would suddenly flip others. One saw a hurried leg, an arm that shone and vanished, a bosom that fled shyly again, an audacious swan, a Leda who was thoroughly enjoying herself and had never heard of virtue. His look suggested that he thought better of one than to suppose that one was not interested in the nude. 'M'sieu,' he seemed to say, with his fixed, brown-eyed regard, 'this is indeed a leg, an authentic leg, not disguised by even the littlest of stockings; it is arranged precisely as M'sieu would desire it.' His sorrow as he went away was dignified with a regret for an inartistic gentleman. One was *en garçon*, and yet one would not look at one's postcards! One had better then cease to be an artist and take to peddling onions and asparagus as the vulgar do.

It was all a long time ago, and now, somehow, the savour had departed from these things. Perhaps he had seen them too often. Perhaps a kind of public surreptitiousness, a quite open furtiveness, had troubled him. Maybe he was not well. He sat at his Café, three quarters down the Boulevard, and before him a multitude of grotesque beings were pacing as he sipped his bock.

Good manners decreed that he should not stare too steadfastly, and he was one who obeyed these delicate dictations. Alas! he was one who obeyed all dictations. For him authority wore a halo, and many sins which his heyday ought to have committed had been left undone only because they were not sanctioned by immediate social usage. He was often saddened when he thought of the things he had not done. It was the only sadness to which he had access, because the evil deeds which he had committed were of so tepid and hygenic a character that they could not be mourned for without hypocrisy; and now that he was released from all privileged restraints and overlookings and could do whatever he wished, he had no wish to do anything.

His wife had been dead for over a year. He had hungered, he had prayed for her death. He had hated that woman (and for how many years!) with a kind of masked ferocity. How often he had been tempted to kill her or to kill himself! How often he had dreamed that she had run away from him or that he had run away from her! He had invented Russian Princes, and Music Hall Stars, and American Billionaires with whom she could adequately elope, and he had both loved and loathed the prospect. What unending, slow quarrels they had together! How her voice had droned pitilessly on his ears! She in one room, he in another, and through the open door there rolled that unending recitation of woes and reproaches, an interminable catalogue of nothings, while he sat dumb as a fish, with a mind that smouldered or blazed. He had stood unseen with a hammer, a poker, a razor in his hand, on tiptoe to do it. A movement, a rush, one silent rush and it was done! He had revelled in her murder. He had caressed it, rehearsed it, relished it, had jerked her head back, and hacked, and listened to her entreaties bubbling through blood!

And then she died! When he stood by her bed he had wished to taunt her, but he could not do it. He read in her eyes—I am dying, and in a little time I shall have vanished like dust on the wind, but you will still be here, and you will never see me again.— He wished to ratify that, to assure her that it was actually so, to say that he would come home on the morrow night, and she would not be there, and that he would return home every night, and she would never be there. But he could not say it. Somehow the words, although he desired them, would not come. His arm went to her neck and settled there. His hand caressed her hair, her cheek. He kissed her eyes, her lips, her languid hands; and the words that came were only an infantile babble of regrets and apologies, assurances that he did love her, that he had never loved any one before, and never would love any one again. . .

Everyone who passed looked into the Café where he sat. Every one who passed looked at him. There were men with sallow faces and wide black hats. Some had hair that flapped about them in the wind, and from their locks one gathered, with some distaste, the spices of Araby. Some had cravats that fluttered and fell and rose again like banners in a storm. There were men with severe, spade-shaped, most responsible-looking beards, and quizzical little eyes which gave the lie to their hairy sedateness— eyes which had spent long years in looking sidewards as a woman passed. There were men of every stage of foppishness—men who had spent so much time on their moustaches that they had only a little left for their finger-nails, but their moustaches exonerated them; others who were coated to happiness, trousered to grotesqueness, and booted to misery. He thought—In this city the men wear their own coats, but they all wear some one else's trousers, and their boots are syndicated.

He saw no person who was self-intent. They were all deeply conscious, not of themselves, but of each other. They were all looking at each other. They were all looking at him; and he returned the severe, or humorous, or appraising gaze of each with a look nicely proportioned to the passer, giving back exactly what was given to him, and no more. He did not stare, for nobody stared. He just looked and looked away, and was as mannerly as was required.

A negro went by arm in arm with a girl who was so sallow that she was only white by courtesy. He was a bulky man, and as he bent greedily over his companion it was evident that to him she was whiter than the snow of a single night.

Women went past in multitudes, and he knew the

appearance of them all. How many times he had watched them or their duplicates striding and mincing and bounding by, each moving like an animated note of interrogation! They were long, and medium, and short. There were women of a thinness beyond comparison, sheathed in skirts as featly as a rapier in a scabbard. There were women of a monumental, a mighty fatness, who billowed and rolled in multitudinous, stormy garments. There were slow eyes that drooped on one as heavily as a hand, and quick ones that stabbed and withdrew, and glanced again appealingly, and slid away cursing. There were some who lounged with a false sedateness, and some who fluttered in an equally false timidity. Some wore velvet shoes without heels. Some had shoes, the heels whereof were of such inordinate length that the wearers looked as though they were perched on stilts and would topple to perdition if their skill failed for an instant. They passed and they looked at him; and from each, after the due regard, he looked away to the next in interminable procession.

There were faces also to be looked at: round chubby faces wherefrom the eyes of oxen stared in slow, involved rumination. Long faces that were keener than hatchets and as cruel. Faces that pretended to be scornful and were only piteous. Faces contrived to ape a temperament other than their own. Raddled faces with heavy eyes and rouged lips. Ragged lips that had been chewed by every mad dog in the world. What lips there were everywhere! Bright scarlet splashes in dead-white faces. Thin red gashes that suggested rat-traps instead of kisses. Bulbous, flabby lips that would wobble and shiver if attention failed them. Lips of a horrid fascination that one looked at and hated and ran to. Looking at him slyly or boldly, they passed along, and turned after a while and repassed him, and turned again in promenade.

He had a sickness of them all. There had been a time when these were among the things he mourned for not having done, but that time was long past. He guessed at their pleasures, and knew them to be without salt. Life, said he, is as unpleasant as a plate of cold porridge. Somehow the world was growing empty for him. He wondered was he outgrowing his illusions, or his appetites, or both? The things in which other men took such interest were drifting beyond him, and (for it seemed that the law of compensation can fail) nothing was drifting towards him in recompense. He foresaw himself as a box with nothing inside it, and he thought—it is not through love or fear or distress that men commit suicide: it is because they have become empty: both the gods and the devils have deserted them and they can no longer support that solemn stagnation. He marvelled to see with what activity men and women played the most savourless of games! With what zest of pursuit they tracked what petty interests. He saw them as ants scurrying with scraps of straw, or apes that pick up and drop and pick again, and he marvelled from what fount they renewed themselves, or with what charms they exorcised the demons of satiety.

On this night life did not seem worth while. The taste had gone from his mouth; his bock was water vilely coloured; his cigarette was a hot stench. And yet a full moon was peeping in the trees along the path, and not far away, where the country-side bowed in silver quietude, the rivers ran through undistinguishable fields chanting their lonely songs. The seas leaped and withdrew, and called again to the stars, and gathered in ecstasy and roared skywards, and the trees did not rob each other more than was absolutely necessary. The men and women were all hidden away, sleeping in their cells, where the moon could not see them, nor the clean wind, nor the stars. They were sundered for a little while from their eternal arithmetic. The grasping hands were lying as quietly as the paws of a sleeping dog. Those eyes held no further speculation than the eyes of an ox who lies down. The tongues that had lied all day, and been treacherous and obscene and respectful by easy turn, said nothing more; and he thought it was very good that they were all hidden, and that for a little time the world might swing darkly with the moon in its own wide circle and its silence.

He paid for his bock, gave the waiter a tip, touched his hat to a lady by sex and a gentleman by clothing, and strolled back to his room that was little, his candle that was three-quarters consumed, and his picture which might be admired when he was dead but which he would never be praised for painting; and, after sticking his foot through the canvas, he tugged himself to bed, agreeing to commence the following morning just as he had the previous one, and the one before that, and the one before that again.

Three Women Who Wept

I

He was one of those men who can call ladies by their Christian names. One day he met twenty-four duchesses walking on a red carpet, and he winked at them, and they were all delighted. It was so at first he appeared to her. Has a mere girl any protection against a man of that quality? and she was the very merest of girls—she knew it. It was not that she was ignorant, for she had read widely about men, and she had three brothers as to whom she knew divers intimate things.

The girl who has been reared among brothers has few defences against other males. She has acquired two things—a belief in the divine right of man, and a curiosity as to what those men are like who are not her brothers. She may love her brothers, but she cannot believe that they adequately represent the other sex. Does not every girl wish to marry the antithesis of her brother? The feeling is that one should marry as far outside of the family as is possible, and as far outside of one's self as may be; but love has become subject to geography, and our choice is often bounded by the tram-line upon which we travel from our houses to our businesses and back again.

While she loved and understood her brothers, she had not in the least understood or believed in the stories she had read, and so, when the Young Man out of a Book came to her, she was delighted but perplexed.

It was difficult to live up to him worthily. It was difficult to know what he would do next, and it was exceedingly difficult to keep out of his way; for, indeed, he seemed to pervade the part of the world where she lived. He was as ubiquitous as the air of the sky. If she went into a shop, he was pacing on the pavement when she came out. If she went for a walk, he was standing at the place farther than which she had decided not to go. She had found him examining a waterfall on the Dodder, leaning over the bear-pit in the Zoological Gardens, and kneeling beside her in the chapel, and her sleep had been distressed by the reflection that maybe he was sitting on her window-sill like a sad sparrow drenched in the rain, all its feathers on end with the cold, and its eyes wide open staring at misery.

The first time they met he spoke to her. He plucked a handkerchief from somewhere and thrust it into her hand, saying—

'You have dropped this, I think' —and she had been too alarmed to disown it.

It was a mighty handkerchief. It was so big that it would scarcely fit into her muff.

'It is a table-cloth,' said she, as she solemnly stuff-

ed away its lengthy flaps. 'It is his own,' she thought
a moment later, and she would have laughed like a
mad woman, only that she had no time, for he was
pacing delicately by her side, and talking in a low
voice that was partly a whisper and partly a whistle,
and was entirely and disturbingly delicious.

The next time they met very suddenly. Scarcely
a dozen paces separated them. She could see him
advancing towards her, and knew by his knitted
brows that he was searching anxiously for something to say. When they drew together he lifted his
hat and murmured—

'How is your handkerchief to-day?'

The query so astonished her that (the verb is her
own) she simply bawled with laughter. From that
moment he treated her with freedom, for if once
you laugh with a person you admit him to equality,
you have ranked him definitely as a vertebrate, your
hand is his by right of species, scarcely can you withhold even your lips from his advances.

Another, a strange, a fascinating thing, was that
he was afraid of her. It was inconceivable, it was
mad, but it was true. He looked at her with disguised terror. His bravado was the slenderest mask.
Every word he said was uttered tentatively, it was
subject to her approval, and if she opposed a statement he dropped it instantly and adopted her alter-
native as one adopts a gift. This astonished her who
had been prepared to be terrified. He kept a little
distance between them as he walked, and when she
looked at him he looked away. She had a vision of
herself as an ogre—whiskers sprouted all over her
face, her ears bulged and swaggled, her voice became
a cavernous rumble, her conversation sounded like

fee-faw-fum—and yet, her brothers were not afraid of her in the least; they pinched her and kicked her hat.

He spoke (but always without prejudice) of the loveliest things imaginable—matters about which brothers had no conception, and for which they would not have any reverence. He said one day that the sky was blue, and, on looking, she found that it was so. The sky was amazingly blue. It had never struck her before, but there was a colour in the firmament before which one might fall down and worship. Sunlight was not the hot glare which it had been: it was rich, generous, it was inexpressibly beautiful. The colour and scent of flowers became more varied. The world emerged as from shrouds and cerements. It was tender and radiant, comeliness lived everywhere, and goodwill. Laughter! the very ground bubbled with it: the grasses waved their hands, the trees danced and curtsied to one another with gentle dignity, and the wind lurched down the path with its hat on the side of its head and its hands in its pockets, whistling like her younger brother.

And then he went away. She did not see him any more. He was not by the waterfall on the Dodder, nor hanging over the bear-pit in the Zoo. He was not in the chapel, nor on the pavement when she came out of a shop. He was not anywhere. She searched, but he was not anywhere. And the sun became the hot pest it had always been: the heavens were stuffed with dirty clouds the way a second-hand shop is stuffed with dirty bundles: the trees were hulking corner-boys with muddy boots: the wind blew dust into her eye, and her brothers pulled her hair and kicked her hat; so that she went apart from all these. She sat before the mirror regarding herself with woeful amazement.

'He was afraid of me!' she said.

And she wept into his monstrous handkerchief.

II

When he came into the world he came howling, and he howled without ceasing for seven long years, except at the times when he happened to be partaking of nourishment, or was fast asleep, and, even then, he snored with a note of defiance and protest which proved that his humour was not for peace.

The time came when he ceased to howl and became fascinated by the problem of how to make other people howl. In this art he became an adept. When he and another child chanced to be left together there came, apparently from the uttermost ends of the earth, a pin, and the other child and the pin were soon in violent and lamentable conjunction.

So he grew.

'Be hanged if I know what to do with him,' said his father as he rebuckled on his belt. 'The devil's self hasn't got the shape or match of such an imp in all the length and breadth of his seven hells. I'm sick, sore and sorry whacking him, so I am, and before long I'll be hung on the head of him. I'm saying that there's more deceit and devilment in his bit of a carcass than there is in a public-house full of tinkers, so there is,'

He turned to his wife—

'It's no credit at all the son you've bore me, ma'm, but a sorrow and a woe that'll be killing us in our old age and maybe damning our souls at the heel of it. Where he got his blackguardly ways from I'm not saying, but it wasn't from my side of the house anyway, so it wasn't, and that's a moral. Get out of my sight you sniffling lout, and if ever I catch you at your practices again I'll lam you till you won't be able to wink without help, so I will.'

'Musha,' sobbed his wife, 'don't be always talking out of you. Any one would think that it was an old criminal thief you were instructing, instead of a bit of a child that'll be growing out of his wildness in no time. Come across to me, child, come over to your mother, my lamb.'

That night, when his father got into bed, he prodded his foot against something under the sheets. Investigation discovered a brown paper bag at the end of the bed. A further search revealed a wasp's nest, inside of which there was a hundred angry wasps blazing for combat. His father left the room with more expedition than decency. He did not stop to put on as much as his hat. He fled to the stream which ran through the meadow at the back of their house, and lay down in it, and in two seconds there was more bad language than water in the stream. Every time he lifted his head for air the wasps flew at him with their tails curled. They kept him there for half an hour, and in that time he laid in the seeds of more rheumatism than could be cured in two lifetimes.

When he returned home he found his wife lying on the floor with a blanket wrapped about her head, groaning by instinct, for she was senseless.

Her face had disappeared. There was nothing where it had been but poisoned lumps. A few days

44

later it was found that she was blind of one eye, and there was danger of erysipelas setting in.

The boy could not be found for some time, but a neighbour, observing a stone come from nowhere in particular and hit a cat, located the first cause in a ditch. He brought the boy home, and grabbed his father just in time to prevent murder being done.

It was soon found that the only thing which eased the restless moaning woman was the touch of her son. All her unmanageable, delirious thoughts centred on him—

'Sure he's only a boy; beating never did good to anything. Give him a chance now for wouldn't a child be a bit wild anyhow. You will be a good boy, won't you? Come to your mother, my lamb.'

So the lad grew, from twelve to fifteen, from fifteen to twenty. Soon he attained to manhood. To his mother he seemed to have leaped in a day from the careless, prattling babe to the responsibly-whiskered miracle at whom mothers sit and laugh in secret delight. This towering, big-footed, hairy person! was he really the little boy who used to hide in her skirts when his father scowled? She had only to close her eyes and she could feel again a pair of little hands clawing at her breast, sore from the violent industry of soft, wee lips.

So he grew. Breeches that were big became small. Bony wrists were continually pushing out of coat cuffs. His feet would burst out of his boots. He grew out of everything but one. A man may outgrow his breeches, he cannot outgrow his nature: his body is never too big or too small to hold that.

Every living thing in the neighbourhood knew him. When a cat saw him coming it climbed a tree and tried to look as much like a lump of wood as it could. When a dog heard his step it tucked its tail out of sight and sought for a hole in the hedge. The birds knew he carried stones in his pockets. No tree cast so black a shadow in the sunlight as he did. There were stories of a bottle of paraffin oil and a cat that screeched in flames. Folk told of a mal-treated dog that pointed its nose to heaven and bay-ed a curse against humanity until a terrified man battered it to death with a shovel. No one knew who did it, but every one said there were only two liv-ing hearts capable of these iniquities—one belonged to the devil, the other to our young man, and they acquitted Satan of the deeds.

The owner of the dog swore by the beasts in the field and the stars in the sky that he would tear the throat out of the man who had injured his beast.

The father drove his one-eyed wife from the house, and went with her to live elsewhere; but she left him and went back to her son, and her husband forswore the twain.

When women saw him in the road they got past him with their breath hissing through their teeth in fear. When men passed him they did it warily, with their fists clenched and their eyes alert. He was shunned by every one. The strength of his arms also was a thing to be afraid of, and in the world there was but two welcomes for him, one from his mother, the other from an old grey rat that slept in his breast—

'Sure, you're all against him,' his mother would say. 'Why don't you give the boy a chance? It's only the hot blood of youth that's working in him—and he never did it either. Look how kind he is to me!

never the bad word or the hard look! Ye black hearts that blame my boy, look among yourselves for the villain. No matter who is against you, come to your mother, my lamb.'

He was found one day at the foot of the cliff with his neck broken. Some said that he had slipped and fallen, some said he had committed suicide, other some pursed their lips tightly and said nothing. All were relieved that he was gone, saving his mother only; she mourned for her only son, and wept bitterly, refusing to be comforted until she died.

III

She had begun to get thin. Her face was growing sharp and peaked. The steady curve of her cheek had become a little indeterminate. Her chin had begun to sag and her eyes to look a little weary. But she had not observed these things, for we do not notice ourselves very much until some other person thinks we are worthy of observation and tells us so; and these changes are so gradual and tiny that we seldom observe them until we awaken for a moment or two in our middle age and then we get ready to fall asleep again.

When her uncle died, the solicitors who had administered his will handed her a small sum of money and intimated that from that date she must hew out her own path in life, and as she had most of the household furniture of her late uncle at her disposal, she decided to let lodgings. Setting about that end with all possible expedition she finished writing 'apartments to let' on a square of pasteboard, and, having placed it prominently in a window, she folded her mittened hands and sat down with some trepidation to await the advent of a lodger.

He came in the night-time with the stars and the moon. He was running like a youthful god, she thought, for her mind had not yet been weaned from certain vanities, and she could not see that a gigantic policeman was in his wake, tracking him with elephantine bounds, and now and again snatching a gasp from hurry to blow furious warnings on a whistle.

It was the sound of the whistle which opened her eyes through her ears. She went to the door and saw him coming framed in the moonlight, his arms pressed tightly to his sides, his head well up and his feet kicking a mile a minute on the pavement. Behind him the whistle shrilled with angry alarm, and the thunder of monumental feet came near as the policeman sprinted in majesty.

As the lodger ran she looked at him. He was a long-legged young man with a pleasant, clean-shaven face. His eyes met hers, and, although he grinned anxiously, she saw that he was frightened. That frightened smile gripped her and she panted noiselessly, 'Oh, run, run!'

As he drew level he fixed his gaze on her, and, stopping suddenly, he ducked under her arm and was inside the house in a twinkling.

The poor lady's inside curled up in fear and had started to uncurl in screams when she felt a hand laid gently on her arm, and, 'Don't make a noise, or I'm caught,' said a voice, whereupon, and with exceeding difficulty, she closed her mouth while the scream went sizzling through her teeth in little gasps. But now the enemy appeared round the corner, tooting incessantly on his whistle, and whacking sparks from the cobblestones as he ran. Behind her she could hear the laboured breathing of a spent runner. The lodger was kneeling at her skirts: he caught her hand and pressed his face against it entreatingly.

The policeman drew near.

'Did you see a fellow skedaddling along here, ma'm?' said he.

She hesitated for only a moment and then, pointing to a laneway opposite, replied—

'He went up there.'

'Thank you, ma'm,' said the policeman with a genial smile, and he sprinted up the laneway whistling cheerily.

She turned to the lodger.

'You had better go now,' said she.

He looked at her ruefully and hesitated.

'If I go now,' he replied, 'I'll be caught and get a month. I'll have to eat skilly, you know, and pick oakum, and get my hair cut.'

She looked at his hair—it was brown and wavy, just at his ears it crisped into tiny curls, and she thought it would be a great pity to cut it. He bore her scrutiny well, with just a trifle of embarrassment and a shyly humorous eye.

'You are the kindest woman I ever met,' said he, 'and I'll never forget you as long as I live. I'll go away now because I wouldn't like to get you into trouble for helping me.'

'What did you do?' she faltered.

'I got into a fight with another man,' he replied, 'and while we were hammering each other the policeman came up. He was going to arrest me, and, before I knew what I was doing, I knocked him down.'

She shook her head.

'You should not have done that. That was very wrong, for he was only doing his duty.'

'I know it,' he admitted, 'but, do you see, I didn't know what I was doing, and then, when I hit him, I got frightened and ran.'

'You poor boy,' said she tenderly.

'And somehow, when I saw you, I knew you wouldn't give me up: wasn't it queer?'

What a nice, gentlemanly young fellow he is, she thought.

'But, of course, I cannot be trespassing on your kindness any longer,' he continued, 'so I'll leave at once, and if ever I get the chance to repay your kindness to a stranger—'

'Perhaps,' said she, 'it might not be quite safe for you to go yet. Come inside and I will give you a cup of tea. You must be worn out with the excitement and the danger. Why, you are shaking all over: a cup of tea will steady your nerves and give him time to stop looking for you.'

'Perhaps,' said he, 'if I turned my coat inside out and turned my trousers up, they wouldn't notice me.'

'We will talk it over,' she replied, with a wise nod.

That was how the lodger came. He told her his name and his employment—he was a bookmaker's clerk. He brought his luggage, consisting mostly of neckties, to her house the following day from his former lodgings.

'Had a terrible time getting away from them,' said

he. 'They rather liked me, you know, and couldn't make out why I wanted to leave.'

'As if you weren't quite free to do as you wished,' quoth his indignant new landlady.

'And then, when they found I would go, they made me pay two weeks' rent in lieu of notice—mean, wasn't it?'

'The low people,' she replied. 'I will not ask you to pay anything this week.'

He put his bandbox on the ground, and shook hands with her.

'You are a brick,' said he, 'the last and the biggest of them. There isn't the like of you in this or any other world, and never was and never will be, world without end, amen.'

'Oh, don't say that,' said she shyly.

'I will,' he replied, 'for it's the truth. I'll hire a sandwichman to stop people in the street and tell it to them. I'll get a week's engagement at the theatre and sing it from the stage. I'll make up a poem about your goodness. I don't know what to do to thank you. Do you see, if I had to pay you now I'd have to pawn something, and I really believe I have pawned everything they'd lend on to get the money for that two weeks' rent. I'm broke until Friday, that's my pay day, but that night I'll come home with my wages piled up on a card.'

'I can lend you a few shillings until then,' said she, laughing.

'Oh no,' said he. 'It's not fair. I couldn't do that,' but he could.

Well the light of the world shone out of the lodger. He was like a sea-breeze in a soap factory. When he awakened in the morning he whistled.

When he came down to breakfast he sang. When he came home in the evening he danced. He had an amazing store of vitality: from the highest hair on the top of his head down to his heels he was alive. His average language was packed with jokes and wonderful curses. He was as chatty as a girl, as good-humoured as a dog, as unconscious as a kitten—and she knew nothing at all of men, except, perhaps that they wore trousers and were not girls. The only man with whom she had ever come in contact was her uncle, and he might have been described as a sniffy old man with a cold; a blend of gruel and grunt, living in an atmosphere of ointment and pills and patent medicine advertisements—and, behold, she was living in unthinkable intimacy with the youngest of young men; not an old, ache-ridden, cough-racked, corn-footed septuagenarian, but a young, fresh-faced, babbling rascal who laughed like the explosion of a blunderbuss, roared songs as long as he was within earshot and danced when he had nothing else to do. He used to show her how to do hand-balances on the arm-chair, and while his boots were cocked up in the air she would grow stiff with terror for his safety and for that of the adjacent crockery.

The first morning she was giving him his breakfast, intending afterwards to have her own meal in the kitchen but he used language of such strangely attractive ferocity, and glared at her with such a humorously-mad eye that she was compelled to breakfast with him.

At night, when he returned to his tea, he swore by this and by that he would die of hunger unless she ate with him; and then he told her all the doings of the day, the bets that had been made and lost, and what sort of a man his boss was, and he extolled the goodness of his friends, and lectured on the vast iniquity of his enemies.

So things went until she was as intimate with him as if he had been her brother. One night he came home just a trifle tipsy. She noted at last what was wrong with him, and her heart yearned over the sinner. There were five or six glasses inside of him, and each was the father of an antic. He was an opera company, a gymnasium, and a menagerie at once, all tinged with a certain hilarious unsteadiness which was fascinating. But at last he got to his bed, which was more than she did.

She sat through the remainder of the night listening to the growth of her half-starved heart. Oh, but there was a warmth there now. . .! Springtime and the moon in flood. What new leaves are these which the trees put forth? Bird, singing at the peep of morn, where gottest thou thy song? Be still, be still, thou stranger, fluttering a wing at my breast. . .

At the end of a month the gods moved, and when the gods move they trample mortals in the dust.

The lodger's employer left Dublin for London, taking his clerk with him.

'Good-bye,' said he.

'Good-bye,' she replied, 'and a pleasant journey to you.'

And she took the card with 'Apartments to Let' written upon it and placed it carefully in the window, and then, folding her mittened hands, she sat down to await the coming of another lodger, and as she sat she wept bitterly.

The Triangle

Nothing is true for ever. A man and a fact will become equally decrepit and will tumble in the same ditch, for truth is as mortal as man, and both are outlived by the tortoise and the crow.

To say that two is company and three is a crowd is to make a very temporary statement. After a short time satiety or use and wont has crept sunderingly between the two, and, if they are any company at all, they are bad company, who pray discreetly but passionately for the crowd which is censured by the proverb.

If there had not been a serpent in the Garden of Eden it is likely that the bored inhabitants of Paradise would have been forced to import one from the outside wilds merely to relax the tedium of a too-sustained duet. There ought to be a law that when a man and a woman have been married for a year they should be forcibly separated for another year. In the meantime, as our lawgivers have no sense, we will continue to invoke the serpent.

Mrs. Mary Morrissy had been married for quite a

time to a gentleman of respectable mentality, a sufficiency of money, and a surplus of leisure—Good things? We would say so if we dared, for we are growing old and suspicious of all appearances, and we do not easily recognise what is bad or good. Beyond the social circumference we are confronted with a debatable ground where good and bad are so merged that we cannot distinguish the one from the other. To her husband's mental attainments (from no precipitate, dizzy peaks did he stare; it was only a tiny plain with the tiniest of hills in the centre) Mrs. Morrissy extended a courtesy entirely unmixed with awe. For his money she extended a hand which could still thrill to an unaccustomed prodigality, but for his leisure (and it was illimitable) she could find no possible use.

The quality of permanency in a transient world is terrifying. A permanent husband is a bore, and we do not know what to do with him. He cannot be put on a shelf. He cannot be hung on a nail. He will not go out of the house. There is no escape from him, and he is always the same. A smile of a certain dimension, moustaches of this inevitable measurement, hands that waggle and flop like those of automata—these are his. He eats this way and he drinks that way, and he will continue to do so until he stiffens into the ultimate quietude. He snores on this note, he laughs on that, dissonant, unescapable, unchanging. This is the way he walks, and he does not know how to run. A predictable beast indeed! He is known inside and out, catalogued, ticketed, and he cannot be packed away.

Mrs. Morrissy did not yet commune with herself about it, but if her grievance was anonymous it was not unknown. There is a back-door to every mind as to every house, and although she refused it house-room, the knowledge sat on her very hearth-stone whistling for recognition.

Indeed, she could not look anywhere without seeing her husband. He was included in every land-scape. His moustaches and the sun rose together. His pyjamas dawned with the moon. When the sea roared so did he, and he whispered with the river and the wind. He was in the picture but was out of drawing. He was in the song but was out of tune. He agitated her dully, surreptitiously, unceasingly. She questioned of space in a whisper—'Are we glued to-gether?' said she. There was a bee in a flower, a burly rascal who did not care a rap for any one; he sat enjoying himself in a scented and gorgeous palace, and in him she confided:

'If,' said she to the bee, 'If that man doesn't stop talking to me I'll kick him. I'll stick a pin in him if he does not go out for a walk.'

She grew desperately nervous. She was afraid that if she looked at him any longer she would see him. To-morrow, she thought, I may notice that he is a short, fat man in spectacles, and that will be the end of everything. But the end of everything is also the beginning of everything, and so she was one half in fear and the other half in hope. A little more and she would hate him, and would begin the world again with the same little hope and the same little despair for her meagre capital.

She had already elaborated a theory that man was intended to work, and that male sloth was off-ensive to Providence and should be forbidden by the law. At times her tongue thrilled, silently as yet, to certain dicta of the experienced Aunt who had superintended her youth, to the intent that a lazy man is a nuisance to himself and to everybody else; and, at last, she disguised this saying as an anecdote and repeated it pleasantly to her husband.

He received it coldly, pondered it with disfavour, and dismissed it by arguing that her Aunt had whiskers, that a whiskered female is a freak, and that the intellectual exercises of a freak are — He lifted his eyebrows and his shoulders. He brushed her Aunt from the tips of his fingers and blew her delicately beyond good manners and the mode.

But time began to hang heavily on both. The intellectual antics of a leisured man become at last wearisome; his methods of thought, by mere familiarity, grow distasteful; the time comes when all the arguments are finished, there is nothing more to be said on any subject, and boredom, without even the covering, apologetic hand, yawns and yawns and cannot be appeased. Thereupon two cease to be company, and even a serpent would be greeted as a cheery and timely visitor. Dismal indeed, and not infrequent, is that time, and the vista therefrom is a long, dull yawn stretching to the horizon and the grave. If at any time we do revalue the values, let us write it down that the person who makes us yawn is a criminal knave, and then we will abolish matrimony and read Plato again.

The serpent arrived one morning hard on Mrs. Morrissy's pathetic pressure. It had three large trunks, a toy terrier, and a volume of verse. The trunks contained dresses, the dog insects, and the book emotion—a sufficiently enlivening trilogy! Miss Sarah O'Malley wore the dresses in exuberant rotation, Mr. Morrissy read the emotional poetry with great admiration, Mrs. Morrissy made friends with the dog, and life at once became complex and joyful.

Mr. Morrissy, exhilarated by the emotional poetry, drew, with an instinct too human to be censured, more and more in the direction of his wife's cousin, and that lady, having a liking for comedy, observed the agile posturings of the gentleman on a verbal summit up and down and around which he flung himself with equal dexterity and satisfaction—crudely, he made puns—and the two were further thrown together by the enforced absences of Mrs. Morrissy, into a privacy more than sealed, by reason of the attentions of a dog who would climb to her lap, and there, with an angry nose, put to no more than temporary rout the nimble guests of his jacket. Shortly Mrs. Morrissy began to look upon the toy terrier with a meditative eye.

It was from one of these, now periodical, retreats that Mrs. Morrissy first observed the rapt attitude of her husband, and instantly life for her became bounding, plentiful, and engrossing.

There is no satisfaction in owning that which nobody else covets. Our silver is no more than second-hand, tarnished metal until some one else speaks of it in terms of envy. Our husbands are barely tolerable until a lady friend has endeavoured to abstract their cloying attentions. Then only do we comprehend that our possessions are unique, beautiful, well worth guarding.

Nobody has yet pointed out that there is an eighth sense; and yet the sense of property is more valuable and more detestable than all the others in combination. The person who owns something is civilised. It is man's escape from wolf and monkeydom. It is individuality at last, or the promise of it, while those other ownerless people must remain either beasts of prey or beasts of burden, grinning with ineffective teeth, or bowing stupid heads for their masters' loads, and all begging humbly for last straws and getting them.

Under a sufficiently equable exterior Mrs. Morrissy's blood was pulsing with greater activity than had ever moved it before. It raced! It flew! At times the tide of it thudded to her head, boomed in her ears, surged in fierce waves against her eyes. Her brain moved with a complexity which would have surprised her had she been capable of remarking upon it. Plot and counterplot! She wove webs horrid as a spider's. She became, without knowing it, a mistress of psychology. She dissected motions and motives. She builded theories precariously upon an eyelash. She pondered and weighed the turning of a head, the handing of a sugar-bowl. She read treason in a laugh, assignations in a song, villainy in a new dress. Deeper and darker things! Profound and vicious depths plunging stark to where the devil lodged in darknesses too dusky for registration! She looked so steadily on these gulfs and murks that at last she could see anything she wished to see; and always, when times were critical, when this and that, abominations indescribable, were separate by no more than a pin's point, she must retire from her watch (alas for a too-sensitive nature!) to chase the enemies of a dog upon which, more than ever, she fixed a meditative eye.

To get that woman out of the house became a

pressing necessity. Her cousin carried with her a baleful atmosphere. She moved cloudy with doubt. There was a diabolic aura about her face, and her hair was red! These things were patent. Was one blind or a fool? A straw will reveal the wind, so will an eyelash, a smile, the carriage of a dress. Ankles also! One saw too much of them. Let it be said then. Teeth and necks were bared too often and too broadly. If modesty was indeed more than a name, then here it was outraged. Shame too! was it only a word? Does one do this and that without even a blush? Even vice should have its good manners, its own decent retirements. If there is nothing else let there be breeding! But at this thing the world might look and understand and censure if it were not brass-browed and stupid. Sneak! Traitress! Serpent! Oh, Serpent! do you slip into our very Eden, looping your sly coils across our flowers, trailing over our beds of narcissus and our budding rose, crawling into our secret arbours and whispering-places and nests of happiness? Do you flaunt and sway your crested head with a new hat on it every day? Oh that my Aunt were here, with the dragon's teeth, and the red breath, and whiskers to match! Here Mrs. Morrissy jumped as if she had been bitten (as indeed she had been) and retired precipitately, eyeing the small dog that frisked about her with an eye almost petrified with meditation.

To get that woman out of the house quickly and without scandal. Not to let her know for a moment, for the blink and twitter of an eyelid, of her triumph. To eject her with ignominy, retaining one's own dignity in the meantime. Never to let her dream of an uneasiness that might have screamed, an anger that could have bitten and scratched and been happy in the primitive exercise. Was such a task beyond her adequacy?

Below in the garden the late sun slanted upon her husband, as with declamatory hands and intense brows he chanted emotional poetry, ready himself on the slope of opportunity to roll into verses from his own resources. He criticised, with agile misconception, the inner meaning, the involved, hardhidden heart of the poet; and the serpent sat before him and nodded. She smiled enchantments at him, and allurements, and subtle, subtle disagreements. On the grass at their feet the toy terrier bounded from his slumbers and curved an imperative and furious hind-leg in the direction of his ear.

Mrs. Morrissy called the dog, and it followed her into the house, frisking joyously. From the kitchen she procured a small basket, and into this she packed some old cloths and pieces of biscuit. Then she picked up the terrier, cuffed it on both sides of the head, popped it into the basket, tucked its humblyagitated tail under its abject ribs, closed the basket, and fastened it with a skewer. She next addressed a label to her cousin's home, tied it to the basket, and despatched a servant with it to the railwaystation, instructing her that it should be paid for on delivery.

At breakfast the following morning her cousin wondered audibly why her little, weeny, tiny pet was not coming for its brecky.

Mrs. Morrissy, with a smile of infinite sweetness, suggested that Miss O'Malley's father would surely feed the brute when it arrived. 'It was a filthy little beast,' said she brightly; and she pushed the toast-rack closer to her husband.

There followed a silence which drowsed and buzzed to eternity, and during which Mr. Morrissy's curled moustaches straightened and grew limp and drooped. An edge of ice stiffened around Miss O'Malley. Incredulity, frozen and wan, thawed into swift comprehension and dismay, lit a flame in her cheeks, throbbed burningly at the lobes of her ears, spread magnetic and prickling over her whole stung body, and ebbed and froze again to immobility. She opposed her cousin's kind eyes with a stony brow.

'I think,' said she, rising, 'that I had better see to my packing.'

'Must you go?' said Mrs. Morrissy, with courteous unconcern, and she helped herself to cream. Her husband glared insanely at a pat of butter, and tried to look like someone who was somewhere else.

Miss O'Malley closed the door behind her with extreme gentleness.

So the matter lay. But the position was unchanged. For a little time peace would reign in that household, but the same driving necessity remained, and before long another, and perhaps more virulent, serpent would have to be requisitioned for the assuagement of those urgent woes. A man's moustaches will arise with the sun; not Joshua could constrain them to the pillow after the lark had sung reveille. A woman will sit pitilessly at the breakfast table however the male eye may shift and quail. It is the business and the art of life to degrade permanencies. Fluidity is existence, there is no other, and for ever the chief attraction of Paradise must be that there is a serpent in it to keep it lively and wholesome. Lacking the serpent we are no longer

in Paradise, we are at home, and our sole entertainment is to yawn when we wish to.

Three Young Wives

She was about to be a mother for the second time, and the fear which is the portion of women was upon her. In a little while she would be in the toils, and she hated and feared physical pain with a great hatred and a great fear. But there was something further which distressed her.

She was a soft, babyish creature, downy and cling-ing, soft-eyed and gentle, the beggar folk had re-ceived gifts at her hand, the dogs knew of her largesse. Men looked on her with approval, and women liked her. Her husband belonged to the type known as 'fine men,' tall, generously-proportioned, with the free and easy joviality which is so common in Ireland. He was born a boy and he would never grow out of that state. The colour of his hair or the wrinkles on his cheek would not have anything to do with his age, for time was powerless against the richness of his blood. He would still be a boy when he was dying of old age; but if protestations, kisses and homage were any criterion, then the fact that he loved his wife was fixed beyond any kind of doubt.

But he did not love her—he was as changeable as the weather of his country. Swift to love, he was equally swift to forget. His passions were of primitive intensity, but they were not steadfast. He clutched with both hands at the present, and was surprised and irritated by the fact that he could in nowise get away from the past: the future he did not care a rap about. Nobody does: there is, indeed, no such thing as the future, there is only the possibility of it, but the past and the present are facts not to be gotten away from. What we have done and what we are doing are things which stamp us, mould us, live with us and after us: what we will do cannot be counted on, has no part in us, has only a problematical existence, and can be interfered with, hindered, nullified or amplified by the thousand unmanageable accidents of futurity.

He had married thanking God from a full heart for His goodness, and believing implicitly that he had plucked the very Flower of Womanhood, and the Heart of the World, and, maybe, he had. There are many Flowers of Womanhood, all equally fragrant, and the Heart of the World can beat against the breast of any man who loves a woman.

Some time previously their little boy had contracted small-pox, and his mother, nursing him took it from him. When they recovered her beauty was gone. The extraordinary bloom which had made her cheek a shrine to worship and marvel at was destroyed for ever, while, by a curious chance, the boy was unmarked.

Now the only love which he had to give was a physical love. He did not love a woman, he loved the husk. Of the woman herself he knew nothing and cared less. He had never sought to know his wife, never tried to pierce beneath her beauty and discover where the woman lived and what she was like at home. Indeed, he knew less of his wife than his servants did, and by little and little she had seen how the matter stood. She had plucked the heart from his mystery and read him to the bones, while remaining herself intact. But she held him still, although by the most primitive and fragile of bonds, by the magnetism of her body, the shining of her eyes, the soft beauty of her cheeks; and, behold! she was undone. The disease had stamped on her face, and, in the recoil, had stamped on her husband's love.

How many nights of solitary tears she had known! she alone could count them, a heavy knowledge. How many slights, shrinkings, coldnesses she had discerned! the tale of them was hot in her brain, the index heavy on her heart.

She knew her loss on the day that her husband looked at her after her recovery when all fear of infection had passed—the stare, the flush, the angry disgust. Her eyes were cameras. She had only to close them and she could see again in dismal procession those dismal details.

And now, as she lay helpless on the bed, she watched him. She was racked with pain, and he was mumbling that it would be all right again in a little time. 'A week from now,' said he, 'and you will have forgotten all about it.'

But she, looking at him with fearful eyes, traced

this sentence at the back of his brain, 'I hope that she will die,' and the life within her which had been sown in happiness and love, and had grown great through misery and tears, was now beating at the gates of entrance. . . She might die: so many people die in labour, and she was not strong. With a new clairvoyant gaze she saw Death standing by the bed, hooded, cloaked and sombre; his eyes were fixed on her, and they were peaceful and kindly eyes. Had there been nothing else to care for she would have gone gladly to the Dark One; but there remained her little son. What heart was he to rest on when she was gone? Whose arms could open so widely as the mother's when he fled from the terrible things which haunt Babyland?—it was an arrow in her heart.

She knew well that her husband would marry again. He was of those men who are inveterate husbands—and that new woman!—Who was she? What was she like? What would be her attitude towards a motherless child? towards her little one? She would be kindly at first, little doubt of that; but afterwards, when her own children came, what would become of the child of a husband's first wife?. . .

She stared down vistas of sorrow. She was a woman, and she knew women. She saw the other little ones, strangers to her, cared for and loved, all their childish troubles the centre of maternal interest and debate, while her boy slunk through a lonely, pathetic childhood, frightened, repressed, perhaps beaten, because he was not of the brood. . .

She saw these things as she lay looking at her husband, and she believed they would come to pass if she died.

And in the night time, when the stars were hidden behind the window curtains, by the light of a lamp that fell on toiling, anxious people, in a hospital-like atmosphere of pain and clamour she did die.

II

It was believed long ago in the ancient kingdom of Erinn that it was death to be a poet, death to love a poet, and death to mock a poet. So the Gael said, and, in that distant time, the people of the Gael were a wise people, holding the ancient knowledge, and they honoured the poet and feared him, for his fostering was among the people of the Shee, and his curse was quickened with the authority of the gods. Even lately the people feared the poets and did them reverence, although the New Ignorance (known humorously as Education) was gradually strangling the life out of Wisdom, and was setting up a different and debased standard of mental values. There was a lady once and she scorned a poet, wittingly and with malice, and it was ill for her in the sequel, for the gods saw to it.

She was very beautiful—'The finest girl in three counties, sir,' said her father: but he might have been prejudiced in favour of his own, and he had been known to speak of himself as 'the finest man in Ireland, and you know what that means, sir.' Further, his dog was 'the greatest dog that ever ratted in the universe.' Whatever he owned was not only good, it was great and unique, and whatever he did not own had, in his opinion, very little to recommend it.

But his daughter was beautiful. When the male

eye encountered her it was in no haste to look away. When the female eye lit on her it was, and the owner of the female eye, having sniffed as was proper, went home and tried to do up her hair or her complexion in the like manner—as was also proper. A great many people believe (and who will quarrel with their verities?) that beauty is largely a matter of craft and adjustment. Such women are beautiful with a little difficulty—they pursue loveliness, run it to earth in a shop, obtain it with a certain amount of minted metal, and reincarnate themselves from a box. They deserve all the success which they undoubtedly obtain. There are other women who are beautiful by accident—such as, the cunning disposition of a dimple, the abilities of a certain kind of smile, the possession of a charming voice—for, indeed, an ugly woman with a beautiful voice is a beautiful woman. But some women are beautiful through the spendthrift generosity of nature, and of this last was she. Whatever of colour, line or motion goes to the construction of beauty that she was heiress to, and she knew it only too well.

A person who has something of his own making may properly be proud of his possession, even if it is nothing more than a stamp album, but a person who has been gifted by Providence or Fairy Godmothers should not be conceited. A self-made man may be proud of his money, but his son may not. Pride in what has been given freely to you is an empty pride, and she was prouder of her beauty than a poet is of his odes—it was her undoing in the end.

She was so accustomed to the homage of men that one who failed to make instant and humble obeisance to her proved himself to be either a very vulgar person or else a miracle. Such folk were few, for the average man bends as readily to beauty as a flower sways to the wind, or the sea to the touch of the moon.

Before she was twenty years of age she had loomed in the eye of every male in her vicinity as the special female whom nature had built to his exclusive measure. When she was twenty-one she had withstood the matrimonial threats of half the male population of Ireland, and she knew how every social grade (there are not many of them) of Irish life made love, for that was the only thing they were able to do while they were near her. From the farmer with a spade in his fist to the landlord with a writ in his agent's pocket, all sang the same song, the sole difference being a matter of grammar; and, although young women have big appetites in these cases, and great recuperative powers, she was as tired of love and love-lorn swains as a young and healthy woman can be, and then, suddenly, and to her own delighted consternation, she did fall in love.

The tantalising part of the whole matter was that she was unable to formulate any good reason for falling in love with this particular male. Her powers of observation (and they were as sharp as a cat's tooth) pointed out that although he was a young man his head was beginning to push out through his hair, and she had always considered that a bald man was outside the pale of human interest. Furthermore, his trousers bagged at the knees, perhaps the most lamentable mishap that can descend on manly apparel. They were often a little jagged at the ends. She did not understand that trousers such as these were the correct usage, they were in the tradition: he was wearing 'the bearded breeches of the bard.' He was a little weak on his legs, and his hands sometimes got in his own way, but she said to herself with a smile, 'How different he is from other men!'

What that difference consisted in got between her and her rest, there was a crumb in her bed on the head of it.

Meanwhile, he had not told her that he loved her, and she was strangely anxious for news to that effect. Indeed, she sought confirmation of her hopes as often as maidenly modesty permitted, which was pretty frequent, for maidenly modesty has its diplomacy also: besides, has not a reigning beauty liberty to pay court?—there are plenty of other queens who have done it.

He was a poet by profession, but his livelihood depended upon his ability as a barrister. When she first saw him he was crossing a street. Suddenly, and in the centre of the road, he halted, with his toes turned in, his fingers caressing his chin, and an expression of rapt and abstracted melancholy on his visage, while he sought for the missing, the transfiguring word. There was a sonnet in his eye and it impeded his vision. Meanwhile, the wheeled traffic of the street addressed language to him which was so vigorous as almost to be poetical. She had pulled him from beneath a horse's head which a frantic driver was endeavouring to pull the mouth from. The words of the driver as he sailed away were—'Go home and die, you moonstruck, gibbering, wobbling omadhaun,' and she had thought that this description was apt and eloquent.

She saw him a second time, when her father took

her for a visit to the Four Courts. He was addressing the Court, and, while his language was magnificent, the judge must have considered that his law was on vacation, for he lost his cause.

They met again in her own home. Her father knew him very well, and, although they seldom met, he had that strong admiration for him which a vigorous and overbearing personality sometimes extends to a shy and unworldly friend.

'A perfect frost as a lawyer,' he used to say, 'but as a poet, sir, Shakespeare is an ass beside him, and if any one asks you who said so, tell them that I did, sir.'

He sat beside her at dinner and forgot her before the first course was removed, and, later, when he knocked a glass off the table, he looked at her as though she was responsible for the debris.

He did not make love to her, a new and remarkable omission in her experience of men, however bald, and while this was refreshing for a time it became intolerable shortly. She challenged him, as a woman can, with the flash of her eyes, the quick music of her laugh, but he was marvelling at the width of the horizon, rapt in contemplation of the distant mountains, observing how a flower poised and nodded on its stalk, following the long, swooping flight of a bird or watching how the moon tramped down on the stars. So far as she could see he was unaware that her charms were of other than average significance.

'These poets are awful fools,' said she angrily.

But the task of awakening this landlocked nature was one which presented many interesting features to her. She was really jealous that he paid her no attention, and, being accustomed to the homage of every male thing over fifteen years of age, she resented his negligence, became interested in him, as every one is in the abnormal, and when a woman becomes interested in a man she is unhappy until he becomes interested in her.

There had arrived, with the express intention of asking her to marry him, another young gentleman. He had a light moustache and a fancy waistcoat, both of which looked new. He was young, rich, handsome, and sufficiently silly to make any woman wish to take charge of him, and her father had told him to 'go in and win, my boy, there's no one I'd like better, sir,' a very good heartener for a slightly dubious youth, even though he may consider that the lady of his choice is watching another man more intently than is pleasant.

The young gentleman gripped, with careful frenzy, at his light, new moustache, and growled as he watched the stalking. But the poet was unoccupied and careless, and then, suddenly, it happened. What movement, conscious or unconscious, opened his eyes one cannot say: the thing seemed to be done without any preliminaries, and he was awakened and in the toils.

They had been reading poetry together, his poetry, and he was expressing, more to himself than to her, how difficult and how delightful it was to work with entire satisfaction within the 'scanty plot' of a sonnet. She was listening with bated breath, and answering with an animation more than slightly tinged with ignorance, for she was as little interested in the making of sonnets as in the making of shoes. Nobody is interested in the making of sonnets, not even poets.

He fell silent after a space and sat gazing at the moon where it globed out on the stillness, and she also became silent. Her nerves, she told herself, were out of order. She was more used to dismissing than to being dismissed, and yet she seemed beaten. There was nothing further that a girl could do. He cared no more about her than he did about whatever woman cleaned his rooms. She was not angry, but a feeling of weariness came upon her. (It is odd that one can be so in earnest when one is in jest.) Once or twice she shook her head at the moon, and as she stared, moody and quiet, it seemed that the moon had slid beyond her vision and she was looking into great caverns of space, bursting with blackness. Some horror of emptiness was reaching to roll her in pits of murk, where her screams would be battered back on her tongue soundless.

With an effort she drew her eyes into focus again and turned them, smiling bitterly, on her companion, and, lo, he was looking at her with timid eyes, amazed eyes, and they spoke, for all their timidity, louder than trumpets. She knew that look—who could mistake it? Here was flame from the authentic fire. He was silent, but his breath came and went hurriedly, and he was bending towards her, little by little he was bending, his eyes, his whole body and soul yearning.

Then she arose—

'It is getting a little cold,' said she: 'we had better go in.'

They went indoors silently. He was walking like a man just awakened from a dream. While she!—her head was high. Where was her equal! She frowned

74

in the face of the moon and stars. She beat her small feet upon the earth and called it slave. She had torn victory from nowhere. A man's head swung at her girdle and she owned the blood that dripped, and her heart tossed rapture and anthem, carol and paean to the air around—she had her hour.

That night the other young gentleman, whom any woman would like to take charge of, asked her to be his wife, and she consented gracefully, slightly disarranging his nice new moustache in the act of surrender.

The next day the poet left the house pleading urgent briefs as an excuse.

'You'll come to the wedding,' cried her father; 'or' (laughing) 'maybe you'll help us with the settlements, that's more in your line,' and he put an arm fondly about his daughter. She, regarding their visitor, nestled to him and laughingly said—

'It would not be like my wedding at all if you stayed away. You must write me an ode,' and her eyes mocked him.

He stood looking at her for a moment, and his eyes mocked also; for the poet knew by his gift what she had done, and he replied with careless scorn—

'I will come with pleasure, and,' with an emphasis, she noted, 'I will dance at your wedding.' So he laughed and marched away heart-whole.

Then, disengaging her arm from her father's, she smiled and walked slowly indoors, and as she walked there spread over her body a fierce coldness, and when her husband sought her afterwards that wintry breast chilled him, and he died: but the poet danced at her wedding, when her eyes were timid, and pleading, and frightened.

III

She read the letter through twice, and then she stood for a few minutes looking in front of her, with her arms hanging loosely by her sides, and her foot tapping on the carpet. She was looking into the future with the thoughtful gaze of one who has cut off all communication with the past, and, with a strange feeling of detachment, she was wondering how that future would reveal itself, and whether he. . .? She crossed to the fireplace, sat down, and read the letter over again.

Her husband had gone out that evening with a friend. In his usual hit-or-miss fashion, he kissed his wife and asked her to settle his tie. He was always asking her to do something, but he never did anything for her. It was, 'Will you hand me the paper, like a good girl?' and, 'I say, dear, my pipe is stuffed, you might stick a hairpin through it,' or, 'You might see, old lady, if there is a match anywhere.' Before their marriage she had been accustomed to men who did things for her, and the change was sudden: likeable enough at first—

. . .How red the fire is to-night! They must be sending better coal than we usually get—there is not a single dark spot in it, and how the shape continually changes! Now it is a deep cave with stalactites hanging from the roof, and little swelling hillocks on the floor, and, over all, a delicate, golden glow surging and fading. The blue flame on the top that flits and flickers like a will-o'-the-wisp is gas, I suppose—I wonder how they extract it. . .I wonder will he be sorry when he comes home, and finds. . .Perhaps his friend will be sufficient for him then. . .It is curious to think of oneself as a piece of animated furniture, a dumb waiter, always ready when required, and decently out of sight when not wanted—not dumb, though! He cannot say I failed to talk about it: but, of course, that is nagging and bad temper, and 'making yourself ridiculous for nothing, my dear.' Nothing! I warned him over and over again; but he must have company. He would be stifled unless he went among men now and again—'Male company is a physical necessity for men, my dear.' I suppose women do not need any other company than that of their husbands, and they must not ask too much of that. . .What strange, careless, hopeful creatures they are, and how they cease to value what they have got! Does the value rise again when it is gone, I wonder?. . .Out all day, and he cannot understand why I ask him to stay with me at night. 'A man wants air, sweetheart.' A woman does not, of course—she would not have the cheek to want anything: there is something not 'nice' about a woman wanting anything. Do all men stifle in the air their wives have breathed? If I ask him 'do you love me still?' he replies, 'of course; do you mind if I run out for an hour or two, dear.' One will ask questions, of course. . .A kiss in the morning, another at night, and, for Heaven's sake, don't bother me in the interval: that is marriage from a man's point of view. Do they really believe that women are alive? Is matrimony always a bondage to them? Are all women's lives so lonely? Are their wishes neglected, their attempts to think laughed at, their pride stricken?—I wonder. . .And he did love me, I know that: but if he has forgotten I must not remember it. He could not see enough of me then: and the things he said, and does not remember—I was a wonder that the world could not equal—it is laughable. A look from me was joy, a word delight, a touch ecstasy. He would run to the ends of the earth to gratify a whim of mine, and life without me was not worth living. . .If I would only love him! If I could only bring myself to care for him a little—he was too humble, too unworthy to imagine—and so forth, and so forth; and it was all true then. Now I am someone who waits upon him. He wants this and that, and asks me for it. He has cut his finger and shouts for me to bind it up, and I must be terribly concerned about it: somehow, he will even manage to blame me for his cut finger. He cannot sleep in the night, so I must awaken also and listen to his complaint. He is sick, and the medicine tastes nasty; I am to understand that if the medicine tastes nasty I am responsible for it—I should not have given him anything nasty: he is surprised: he trusted me not to do such a thing to him. He turns to me like a child when he has any. . .he turns to me like a child and trusts. . .he turns to me. . .like a child. . .

The sound of a horse's hooves came to her, and she arose from her chair with frightened haste. She looked swiftly at the clock, and then stood listening in a rigid attitude, with a face that grew white and peaked, and flushed and paled again. The car came swiftly nearer and stopped a little way from the house. Then a foot crunched the gravel, and her desperate eyes went roving quickly about the room as though she were looking for a place to hide in.

Next, after a little interval of silence, a pebble struck the window. She stood for a moment staring at the window and then ran to it, swung open a pane of glass, and, leaning out, she called in a high, strained voice, 'I will not go.' Then, closing the window again, she ran back to the fireplace, crouched down on the rug and pushed her fingers into her ears.

Her husband came home before eleven o'clock, brushed the wraith of a kiss half an inch from her lips, and asked was there anything nice for supper? The supper things were already on the table, and, after tasting a mouthful—

'Who cooked this?' said he.

She was watching him intently.

'The girl did,' she replied.

'I knew it,' said he angrily, 'it's beastly: you might have done it yourself when you were not busy; a lot you care about what I like.'

'I will do it to-morrow,' she replied quietly.

'Yes do,' said he, 'there is no one can cook like you.'

And she, still watching him intently, suddenly began to laugh.

He leaped up from the table and, after a stare of indignant astonishment, he stalked off to bed.

'You are always giggling about nothing,' said he, and he banged the door.

The Horses

He was tall and she was short. He was bulky, promising to be fat. She was thin, and, with a paring here and there, would have been skinny. His face was sternly resolute, solemn indeed; hers was prim, and primness is the most everlasting, indestructible trait of humanity. It can outface the Sphinx. It is destructible only by death. Whoever has married a prim woman must hand over his breeches and his purse, he will collect postage stamps in his old age, he will twiddle his thumbs and smile when the visitor asks him a question, he will grow to dislike beer, and will admit and assert that a man's place is the home— these things come to pass as surely as the procession of the seasons.

It may be asked why he had married her, and it would be difficult to find an answer to that question. The same query might be put to almost any couple, for (and it is possibly right that it should be so) we do not marry by mathematics, but by some extraordinary attraction which is neither entirely sexual nor mental. Something other than these, something as yet uncharted by psychology, is the determining factor. It may be that the universal, strange chemistry of nature, planning granite and twig, ant and onion, is also ordering us more imperatively and more secretly than we are aware.

He had always been a hasty creature. He never had any brains, and had never felt the lack of them. He was one of those men who are called 'strong,' because of their imperfect control over themselves. His appetites and his mental states ruled him. He was impatient of any restraint; whatever he wanted to do he wanted urgently to do and would touch no alternatives. He had the robust good humour which will cheerfully forgive you to-morrow for the wrongs he has done you to-day. He bore no malice to anyone on earth except those who took their medicine badly. Meek people got on very well with him because they behaved themselves, but he did not like them to believe they would inherit the earth.

Some people marry because other people have done so. It is in the air, like clothing and art and not eating with a knife. He, of course, got married because he wanted to, and the singular part of it was that he did not mate with a meek woman. Perhaps he thought she was meek, for before marriage there is a habit of deference on both sides which is misleading and sometimes troublesome.

From the beginning of their marriage he had fought against his wife with steadiness and even ferocity. Scarcely had they been wed when her gently-repressive hand was laid upon him, and, like a startled horse, he bounded at the touch into freedom—that is, as far as the limits of the matrimonial rope would permit. Of course he came back again—there was the rope, and the unfailing, untiring hand easing him to the way he was wanted to go.

There was no fighting against that. Or, at least, it did not seem that fighting was any use. One may punch a bag, but the bag does not mind, and at last one grows weary of unproductive quarrelling. One shrugs one's shoulders, settles to the collar, and accepts whatever destiny the gods, in their wisdom, have ordained. Is life the anvil upon which the gods beat out their will? It is not so. The anvil is matter, the will of the gods is life itself, urging through whatever torment to some identity which it can only surmise or hope for; and the one order to life is that it shall not cease to rebel until it has ceased to live; when, perhaps, it can take up the shaping struggle in some other form or some other place.

But he had almost given in. Practically he had bowed to the new order. Domestic habits were settling about him thick as cobwebs and as clinging. His feet were wiped on the mat when he came in. His hat was hung on the orthodox projection. His kiss was given at the stated time, and lasted for the regulation period. The chimney-corner claimed him and got him. The window was his outlook on life. Beyond the hall door were foreign lands inhabited by people who were no longer of his kind. The cat and the canary, these were his familiars, and his wife was rapidly becoming his friend.

Once a day he trod solemnly forth on the designated walk.

'Be back before one o'clock,' said the voice of kind authority, 'lunch will be ready.'

'Won't you be back before two?' said that voice,

'the lawn has to be rolled.'

'Don't stay out after three,' the voice entreated, 'we are going to visit Aunt Kate.'

And at one and two and three o'clock he paced urgently wifeward. He ate the lunch that was punctually ready. He rolled the inevitable lawn. He trod sturdily to meet the Aunt Kate and did not quail, and then he went home again. One climbed to bed at ten o'clock, one was gently spoken to until eleven o'clock, and then one went to sleep.

On a day she entrusted him with a sum of money, and requested that he should go down the town and pay at certain shops certain bills, the details whereof she furnished to him on paper.

'Be back before three o'clock,' said the good lady, 'for the Fegans are coming to tea. You need not take your umbrella, it won't rain; and you ought to leave your pipe behind, it doesn't look nice. Bring some cigarettes instead, and your walking-stick if you like, and be sure to be back before three.'

He pressed his pipe into a thing on the wall which was meant for pipes, put his cigarette-case into his pocket, and took his walking-stick in his hand.

'You did not kiss me good-bye,' said she gently.

So he returned and did that, and then he went out.

It was a delicious day. The sun was shining with all its might. One could see that it liked shining, and hoped everybody enjoyed its art. If there were birds about anywhere it is certain they were singing. In this suburb, however, there were only sparrows, but they hopped and flew, and flew and hopped, and cocked their heads sideways and chirped something cheerful, but possibly rude, as one passed. They were busy to the full extent of their beings, playing innocent games with happy little flies, and there was not one worry among a thousand of them.

There was a cat lying on a hot window-ledge. She was looking drowsily at the sparrows, and anyone could see that she loved them and wished them well.

There was a dog stretched across a doorway. He was very quiet, but he was not in the least bored. He was taking a sun-bath, and he was watching the cat. So steadily did he observe her that one discerned at a glance he was her friend, and would protect her at any cost.

There was a small boy who held in his left hand a tin can and a piece of string. With his right hand he was making affectionate gestures to the dog. He loved playing with animals, and he always rewarded their trust in him.

Our traveller paced slowly onwards, looking at his feet as he went. He noticed with a little dismay that he could not see as much of his legs as he thought he should see. There was a slight but nicely-shaped curve between him and his past.

'I am getting fat,' said he to himself, and the reflection carried him back to the morning mirror.

'I am getting a bit bald, too,' said he, and a quiet sadness took possession of him.

But he reassured himself. One does get fat. 'Everyone gets fat,' said he, 'after he gets married.' He reviewed his friends and acquaintances, and found that this was true, and he bowed before an immutable decree.

'One does get bald,' quoth he. 'Everybody gets

bald. The wisest people in the world lose their hair. Kings and generals, rich people and poor people, they are all bald! It is not a disgrace,' said he; and he trod soberly forward in the sunshine.

A young man caught up on him from behind, and strode past. He was whistling. His coat-tails were lifted and his hands were thrust in his pockets. His elbows jerked to left and right as he marched.

'A fellow oughtn't to swagger about like that,' said our traveller. 'What does he want to tuck up his coat for, anyhow? It's not decent,' said he in a low voice. 'It makes people laugh,' said he.

A girl came out of a shop nearby and paced down in their direction. She looked at the young man as they passed, and then she turned again, a glance, no more, and looked after him without stopping her pace. She came on. She had no pockets to stick her hands in, but she also was swaggering. There was a left and right movement of her shoulders, an impetus and retreat of her hips. Something very strong and yet reticent about her surging body. She passed the traveller and went down the road.

'She did not look at me,' said he, and his mind folded its hands across its stomach, and sat down, while he went forward in the sunlight to do his errands.

He stopped to light a cigarette, and stood for a few minutes watching the blue smoke drifting and thinning away on the air. While he stood a man drove up with a horse and car. The car was laden with groceries—packets of somebody's tea, boxes of somebody's chocolate, bottles of beer and of mineral water, tins of boot blacking, and parcels of soap; confectionery, and tinned fish, cheese, macaroni, and jam.

The man was beating the horse as he approached, and the traveller looked at them both through a wreath of smoke.

'I wonder,' said he, 'why that man beats his horse?'

The driver was sitting at ease. He was not angry. He was not impatient. There was nothing the matter with him at all. But he was steadily beating the horse; not harshly, gently in truth. He beat the horse without ill-will, almost without knowing he was doing it. It was a sort of wrist exercise. A quick, delicate twitch of the whip that caught the animal under the belly, always in the same place. It was very skilful, but the driver was so proficient in his art that one wondered why he had to practise at it any longer. And the horse did not make any objection! Not even with his ears; they lay back to his mane as he jogged steadily forward in the sunlight. His hooves were shod with iron, but they moved with an unfaltering, humble regularity. His mouth was filled with great yellow teeth, but he kept his mouth shut and one could not see them. He did not increase or diminish his pace under the lash; he jogged onwards, and did not seem to mind it.

The reins were jerked suddenly, and the horse turned into the path and stopped, and when he stood he was not any quieter than when he had been moving. He did not raise his head or whisk his tail. He did not move his ears to the sounds behind and on either side of him. He did not paw and fumble with his feet. There was a swarm of flies about his head; they moved along from the point of his nose to the top of his forehead, but mostly they clustered in black obscene patches about his eyes, and through these patches his eyes looked out with a strange patience, a strange mildness. He was stating a fact over and over to himself, and he could not think of anything else.

'There are no longer any meadows in the world,' said he. 'They came in the night and took away the green meadows, and the horses do not know what to do.' . . .Horse! Horse! Little horse!. . .You do not believe me. There are those who have no whips. There are children who would love to lift you in their arms and stroke your head. . .

The driver came again, he mounted to his seat, and the horse turned carefully and trotted away.

The man with the cigarette looked after them for a few minutes, and then he also turned carefully to do his errands.

He reached the Railway Station and peered in at the clock. There were some men in uniform striding busily about. Three or four people were moving up the steps towards the ticket office. A raggedy man shook a newspaper in his face, paused for half a second, and fled away bawling his news. A red-faced woman pushed hastily past him. She was carrying a big basket and a big baby. She was terribly engrossed by both, and he wondered if she had to drop one which of them it would be. A short, stout, elderly man was hoisting himself and a great leather portmanteau by easy stages up the steps. He was very determined. He bristled at everybody as at an enemy. He regarded inanimate nature as if he was daring it to move. It would not be easy to make that man miss a train. A young lady trod softly up the steps. She draped snowy garments about her, but her ankles rebelled: whoever looked quickly saw them once, and then she spoke very severely to them, and they hid themselves. It was plain that she could scarcely control them, and that they would escape again when she wasn't looking. A young man bounded up the steps; he was too late to see them, and he looked as if he knew it. He stared angrily at the girl, but she lifted her chin slightly and refused to admit that he was alive. A very small boy was trying to push a large indiarubber ball into his mouth, but his mouth was not big enough to hold it, and he wept because of his limitations. He was towed along by his sister, a girl so tall that one might say her legs reached to heaven, and maybe they did.

He looked again at the hour. It was one minute to two o'clock; and then something happened. The whole white world became red. The oldest seas in the world went suddenly lashing into storm. An ocean of blood thundered into his head, and the noise of that primitive flood, roaring from what prehistoric gulfs, deafened him at an instant. The waves whirled his feet from under him. He went foaming up the steps, was swept violently into the ticket office, and was swirled away like a bobbing cork into the train. A guard tried to stop him, for the train was already taking its pace, but one cannot keep out the tide with a ticket-puncher. The guard was overwhelmed, caught in the backwash, and swirled somewhere, anywhere, out of sight and knowledge. The train gathered speed, went flying out of the station into the blazing sunlight, picked up its heels and ran, and ran, and ran; the wind leaped by the carriage window, shrieking with laughter; the wide fields danced with each other, shouting aloud.

'The horses are coming again to the green meadows. Make way, make way for the great wild horses!'

And the trees went leaping from horizon to horizon shrieking and shrieking the news.

from Three Lovers Who Lost

Aloysius Murphy went a-courting when the woods were green. There were grapes in the air and birds in the river. A voice and a song went everywhere, and the voice said, 'Where is my beloved?' and the song replied, 'Thy beloved is awaiting thee, and she stretches her hands abroad and laughs for thy coming; bind then the feather of a bird to thy heel and a red rose upon thy hair, and go quickly.'

So he took his hat from behind the door and his stick from beside the bed and went out into the evening.

He had been engaged to Miss Nora MacMahon for two ecstatic months, and held the opinion that the earth and the heavens were aware of the intensity of his passion, and applauded the unique justice of his choice.

By day he sat humbly in a solicitor's office, or scurried through the thousand offices of the Four Courts, but with night came freedom, and he felt himself to be of the kindred of the gods and march- ed in pomp. By what subterranean workings had he become familiar with the lady? Suffice it that the impossible is possible to a lover. Everything can be achieved in time. The man who wishes to put a mountain in his pocket can do so if his pocket and his wish be of the requisite magnitude.

Now the lady towards whom the raging torrent of his affections had been directed was the daughter of his employer, and this, while it notated romance, pointed also to tragedy. Further, while this fact was well within his knowledge, it was far from the cognisance of the lady. He would have enlightened her on the point, but the longer he delayed the revelation, the more difficult did it become. Perpetually his tongue ached to utter the truth. When he might be squeezing her hand or plunging his glance into the depths of her eyes, consciousness would touch him on the shoulder with a bony hand and say, 'That is the boss's daughter you are hugging'—a reminder which was provocative sometimes of an almost unholy delight, when to sing and dance and go mad was but natural; but at other times it brought with it moods of woe, abysses of blackness.

In the solitude of the room wherein he lodged he sometimes indulged in a small drama, wherein, as the hero, he would smile a slightly sad and quizzical smile, and say gently, 'Child, you are Mr. MacMahon's daughter, I am but his clerk'—here the smile became more sadly quizzical—'how can I ask you to forsake the luxury of a residence in Clontarf for the uncongenial, nay, bleak surroundings of a South Circular Road habitation?' And she, ah me! She vowed that a hut and a crust and the love of her heart. . .! No matter!

So, nightly, Aloysius Murphy took the tram to Clontarf, and there, wide-coated and sombreroed like a mediaeval conspirator, he trod delicately beside his cloaked and hooded inamorata, whispering of the spice of the wind and the great stretches of the sea.

Now a lover who comes with the shades of night, harbinger of the moon, and hand in glove with the stars, must be a very romantic person indeed, and, even if he is not, a lady whose years are tender can easily supply the necessary gauze to tone down his too-rigorous projections. But the bird that flies by night must adduce for our curiosity substantial reason why his flight has deserted the whiteness of the daytime; else we may be tempted to believe that his advent in darkness is thus shrouded for even duskier purposes—Miss MacMahon had begun to inquire who Mr. Murphy was, and he had, accordingly, begun to explain who he was not. This explanation had wrapped his identity in the most labyrinthine mystery, but Miss MacMahon detected in the rapid, incomprehensible fluctuations of his story a heart torn by unmerited misfortune, and whose agony could only be alleviated by laying her own dear head against its turmoil.

To a young girl a confidant is almost as necessary as a lover, and when the rendezvous is clandestine, the youth mysterious, and his hat broad-leafed and flapping, then the necessity for a confidant becomes imperative.

Miss MacMahon confided the knowledge of all her happiness to the thrilled ear of her younger sister, who at once hugged her, and bubbled query, conjecture, and admonishment. '. . .Long or short?

. . .Dark or fair?' '. . .and slender. . .with eyes. . .
dove. . .lightning. . .hair. . .and so gentle. . .and then
I said. . .and then he said. . .!' 'Oh, sweet!' sighed
the younger sister, and she stretched her arms wide
and crushed the absent excellences of Mr. Murphy
to her youthful breast.

On returning next day from church, having listened awe-stricken to a sermon on filial obedience, the
little sister bound her mother to secrecy, told the
story, and said she wished she were dead. Sub-
sequently the father of Clann MacMahon was informed, and he said 'Hum' and 'Ha,' and rolled a
fierce, hard eye, and many times during the progress
of the narrative he interjected with furious energy
these words, 'Don't be a fool, Jane,' and Mrs.
MacMahon responded meekly, 'Yes, dear,' and Mr.
MacMahon then said 'Hum' and 'Ha' and 'Gr-r-r-up'
in a truly terrible and ogreish manner; and in her
distant chamber Miss MacMahon heard the rever-
beration of that sonorous grunt, and whispered to
her little sister, 'Pa's in a wax,' and the little sister
pretended to be asleep.

The spectacle of an elderly gentleman, side-
whiskered, precise and grey, disguising himself with
mufflers and a squash hat, and stalking with sombre
fortitude the erratic wanderings of a pair of young
feather-heads, is one which mirth may be pleased
to linger upon. Such a spectacle was now to be observed in the semi-rural outskirts of Clontarf. Mr.
MacMahon tracked his daughter with considerable
stealth, adopting unconsciously the elongated and
nervous stride of a theatrical villain. He saw her
meet a young man wearing a broad-brimmed hat,
whose clothing was mysteriously theatrical, and

whose general shape, when it could be glimpsed, was oddly familiar.

'I have seen that fellow somewhere,' said he.

The lovers met and kissed, and the glaring father spoke rapidly but softly to himself for a few moments. He was not accustomed to walking, and it appeared as if these two intended to walk for ever, but he kept them in sight, and when the time came for parting he was close at hand.

The parting was prolonged, and renewed, and rehearsed again with amendments and additions: he could not have believed that saying good-bye to a person could be turned into so complicated and symbolic a ceremony; but at last his daughter, with many a backward look and wave of hand, departed in one direction, and the gentleman, after similar signals, moved towards the tramway.

'I know that fellow, whoever he is,' said Mr. MacMahon.

Passing a lamp-post, Mr. Aloysius Murphy stayed for a moment to light his pipe, and Mr. MacMahon stared, he ground his teeth, he foamed at the mouth, and his already prominent eyes bulged still further and rounder.

'Well, I'm—!' said he.

He turned and walked homewards slowly, murmuring often to himself and to the night, 'All right! wait, though! Hum! Ha! Gr-r-r-up!'

That night he repeatedly entreated his wife 'Not to be a fool, Jane,' and she as repeatedly replied, 'Yes, dear.' Long after midnight he awoke her by roaring violently from the very interior depths of a dream, 'Cheek of the fellow! Pup! Gr-r-r-up!'

At breakfast on the following morning he suggested to his wife and elder daughter that they should visit his office later on in the day.

'You have never seen it, Nora,' said he, 'and you ought to have a look at the den where your poor old daddy spends his time grinding dress material for his family from the faces of the poor. I've got some funny clerks, too: one of them is a curiosity.' Here, growing suddenly furious he gave an egg a clout.

His daughter giggled.

'Oh, Pa,' said she, 'you are not breaking that egg, you are murdering it.'

He looked at her gloomily.

'It wasn't the egg I was hitting,' said he 'Gr-r-r-up,' said he suddenly, and he stabbed a piece of butter, squashed it to death on a slice of bread, and tore it to pieces with his teeth.

The young lady looked at him with some amazement, but she said nothing, for she believed, as most ladies do, that men are a little mad sometimes, and are foolish always.

Her father intercepted that glance, and instantly snarled.

'Can you cook, young woman?' said he.

'Of course, father,' replied the perplexed maiden.

He laid aside his spoon and gave her his full attention.

'Can you cook potatoes?' said he. 'Can you mash 'em, eh? Can you mash 'em? What! You can. They call them Murphies in this country, girl. Can you mash Murphys, eh? I can. There's a Murphy I know, and, although it's been mashed already, by the Lord Harry I'll mash it again. Did you ever know that potatoes had eyes, Miss? Did you ever notice it

when you were cooking them? Did you ever look
into the eyes of a Murphy, eh? When you mashed
it—what? Don't answer me, girl.'

'I don't know what you are talking about, Pa,'
said the young lady.

'Don't you, now?' grinned the furious gentle
man, and his bulging eyes looked like little round
balls of glass. 'Who said you did, Miss? Gr-r-r-up,'
said he, and the poor girl jumped as though she had
been prodded with a pin.

Mr. Aloysius Murphy's activities began at ten
o'clock in the morning by opening the office letters
with an ivory instrument and handing them to his
employer; then, as each letter was read, he entered
its receipt and date in a book kept for that pur
pose.

When Mr. MacMahon came in on the morning
following the occurrences I have detailed he neglect
ed, for the first time in many years, to respond to
his clerk's respectfully-cordial salutation. To the
discreet 'Good-morning, sir,' he vouchsafed no
reply. Mr. Murphy was a trifle indignant and a good
deal perturbed, for to an unquiet conscience a
word or the lack of it is a goad. Once or twice,
looking up from his book, he discovered his em
ployer's hard eyes fixed upon him with a regard too
particular to be pleasant.

An employer seldom does more than glance at his
clerk, just the sideward glint of a look which re
marks his presence without admitting his necessity,
and in return the clerk slants a hurried eye on his
employer, notes swiftly if his aspect be sulky or
benign, and stays his vision at that. But, now Mr
Murphy, with sudden trepidation, with a frightful

inking in the pit of his stomach, became aware that his employer was looking at him stealthily; and, little by little, he took to sneaking glances at his employer. After a few moments neither seemed to be able to keep his eyes from straying—they created opportunities in connection with the letters; the one looking intent, wide-eyed, and with a cold, rigid, rigid, hard stare, and the other scurrying and furtive, in-and-away, hit-and-miss-and-try-again, wink, blink, and twitter.

Mr. MacMahon spoke.

'Murphy!'

'Yes, sir.'

'Have you anything in Court to-day?'

'Yes, sir, an ex parte application, Donald and Cluggs.'

'Let O'Neill attend to it. I shall want you to draft a deed for some ladies who will call here at noon. You can come down at ten minutes after twelve.'

'Yes, sir,' said Murphy.

He grabbed his share of the letters and got to the door bathed in perspiration and forebodings. He closed the door softly behind him, and stood for a few seconds staring at the handle. 'Blow you!' said he viciously to nothing in particular, and he went slowly upstairs.

'He can't know,' said he on the first landing. On the second floor he thought, 'She couldn't have told for she didn't know herself.' He reached his desk, 'I wish I had a half of whisky,' said the young man to himself.

Before, however, twelve o'clock arrived he had journeyed on the hopeful pinions of youth from the dogmatic 'could not be' to the equally immovable 'is not,' and his mind resumed its interrupted equilibrium.

At twelve o'clock Mrs. and Miss MacMahon arrived and were at once shown into the private office. At ten minutes past, Mr. Murphy's respectful tap was heard. 'Don't, Eddie,' said Mrs. MacMahon in a queer, flurried voice. 'Come in,' said her husband. Nora was examining some judicial cartoons pinned over the mantelpiece. Mr. Murphy opened the door a few inches, slid through the aperture, and was at once caught and held by his employer's eye, which, like a hand, guided him to the table with his notebook. Under the almost physical pressure of that authoritative glare he did not dare to look who was in the room, but the rim of his eye saw the movement of a skirt like the far-away shadowy canter of a ghost's robe. He fixed his attention on his notebook.

Mr. MacMahon began to dictate a Deed of Conveyance from a precedent deed in his hand. After dictating for some few minutes—

'Murphy,' said he, and at the word the young lady studying the cartoons stiffened, 'I've rather lost the thread of that clause; please read what you have down'

Murphy began to read, and at the first word the girl made a tiny, shrill, mouse's noise, and then stood stock-still, tightened up and frightened, with her two wild eyes trying to peep around her ears.

Mr. Murphy heard the noise and faltered—he knew instinctively. Something told him with the bellowing assurance of a cannon who was there. He must look. He forced his slack face past the granite image that was his employer, saw a serge-clad figure that he knew, one ear and the curve of a cheek. Then a cascade broke inside his head. It buzzed and chattered and crashed, with now and again the blank brutality of thunder bashing through the noise. The serge-clad figure swelled suddenly to a tremendous magnitude, and then it receded just as swiftly, and the vast earth spun minutely on a pin's point ten million miles away, and she was behind it, her eyes piercing with scorn. . .Through the furious winds that whirled about his brain he heard a whisper, thin and cold, and insistent as a razor's edge, 'Go on, Murphy; go on, Murphy.' He strove to fix his attention on his shorthand notes—to fight it down, to stand the shock like a man, and then crawl into a hole somewhere and die; but his mind would not grip, nor his eyes focus. The only words which his empty brain could pump up were these, irrelevant and idiotic, "'A frog he would a-wooing go, heigho,' said Rowley"; and they must not be said. 'It is a bit difficult, perhaps,' said the whispering voice that crept through the tumult of winds and waters in his head. 'Never mind, take down the rest of it, and the far-away whisper began to say things all about nothing, making queer little noises and pauses, running for a moment into a ripple of sound, and eddying and dying away and coming back again—buz-z-z! His note-book lying on the table was as small as a postage stamp, while the pencil in his hand was as big as an elephant's leg. How can a man write on a microscopic blur with the stump of a fir tree? He poked and prodded, and Mr. MacMahon watched for a few moments his clerk poking his note-book with the wrong end of a pencil. He silently pulled his daughter forward and made her look. After a little—

'That will do, Murphy,' said he, and Mr. Murphy, before he got out, made two severe attempts to walk through a wall.

For half an hour he sat at his desk in a trance, with his eyes fixed upon an ink-bottle. At last, nodding his head slowly—

'I'll bet you a shilling,' said he to the ink-bottle, 'that I get the sack to-night.'

And the ink-bottle lost the wager.

The Blind Man

He was one who would have passed by the Sphinx without seeing it. He did not believe in the necessity for sphinxes, or in their reality, for that matter—they did not exist for him. Indeed, he was one to whom the Sphinx would not have been visible. He might have eyed it and noted a certain bulk of grotesque stone, but nothing more significant.

He was sex-blind, and, so, peculiarly limited by the fact that he could not appreciate women. If he had been pressed for a theory or metaphysic of womanhood he would have been unable to formulate any. Their presence he admitted, perforce: their utility was quite apparent to him on the surface, but, subterraneously, he doubted both their existence and their utility. He might have said perplexedly—why cannot they do whatever they have to do without being always in the way? He might have said—Hang it, they are everywhere, and what good are they doing? They bothered him, they destroyed his ease when he was near them, and they spoke a language which he did not understand

and did not want to understand. But as his limitations did not press on him neither did they trouble him. He was not sexually deficient, and he did not dislike women; he simply ignored them, and was only really at home with men. All the crudities which we enumerate as masculine delighted him—simple things, for, in the gender of abstract ideas, vice is feminine, brutality is masculine, the female being older, vastly older than the male, much more competent in every way, stronger, even in her physique, than he, and, having little baggage of mental or ethical preoccupations to delay her progress, she is still the guardian of evolution, requiring little more from man than to be stroked and petted for a while.

He could be brutal at times. He liked to get drunk at seasonable periods. He would cheerfully break a head or a window, and would bandage the one damage or pay for the other with equal skill and pleasure. He liked to tramp rugged miles swinging his arms and whistling as he went, and he could sit for hours by the side of a ditch thinking thoughts without words—an easy and a pleasant way of thinking, and one which may lead to something in the long run.

Even his mother was an abstraction to him. He was kind to her so far as doing things went, but he looked over her, or round her, and marched away and forgot her.

Sex-blindness carries with it many other darknesses. We do not know what masculine thing is projected by the feminine consciousness, and civilisation, even life itself, must stand at a halt until that has been discovered or created; but art is the female projected by the male: science is the male projected by the male—as yet a poor thing, and to remain so until it has become art; that is, has become fertilised and so more psychological than mechanical. The small part of science which came to his notice (inventions, machinery, etc.) was easily and delightedly comprehended by him. He could do intricate things with a knife and a piece of string, or a hammer and a saw; but a picture, a poem, a statue, a piece of music—these left him as uninterested as they found him: more so, in truth, for they left him bored and dejected.

His mother came to dislike him, and there were many causes and many justifications for her dislike. She was an orderly, busy, competent woman, the counterpart of endless millions of her sex, who liked to understand what she saw or felt, and who had no happiness in reading riddles. To her he was at times an enigma, and at times again a simpleton. In both aspects he displeased and embarrassed her. One has one's sense of property, and in him she could not put her finger on anything that was hers. We demand continuity, logic in other words, but between her son and herself there was a gulf fixed, spanned by no bridge whatever; there was complete isolation; no boat plied between them at all. All the kindly human things which she loved were unintelligible to him, and his coarse pleasures or blunt evasions distressed and bewildered her. When she spoke to him he gaped or yawned; and yet she did not speak on weighty matters, just the necessary small-change of existence—somebody's cold, somebody's dress, somebody's marriage or death. When she addressed him on sterner subjects, the ground, the weather, the crops, he looked at her as if she were a baby, he listened with stubborn resentment and strode away a confessed boor. There was no contact anywhere between them, and he was a slow exasperation to her—What can we do with that which is ours and not ours? Either we own a thing or we do not, and, whichever way it goes, there is some end to it; but certain enigmas are illegitimate and are so hounded from decent cogitation.

She could do nothing but dismiss him, and she could not even do that, for there he was at the required periods, always primed with the wrong reply to any question, the wrong aspiration, the wrong conjecture; a perpetual trampler on mental corns, a person for whom one could do nothing but apologise.

They lived on a small farm, and almost the entire work of the place was done by him. His younger brother assisted, but that assistance could have easily been done without. If the cattle were sick, he cured them almost by instinct. If the horse was lame or wanted a new shoe, he knew precisely what to do in both events. When the time came for ploughing, he gripped the handles and drove a furrow which was as straight and as economical as any furrow in the world. He could dig all day long and be happy; he gathered in the harvest as another would gather in a bride; and, in the intervals between these occupations, he fled to the nearest public house and wallowed among his kind.

He did not fly away to drink; he fled to be among men—then he awakened. His tongue worked with the best of them, and adequately too. He could speak weightily on many things—boxing, wrestling, hunting, fishing, the seasons, the weather, and the chances of this and the other man's crops. He had deep knowledge about brands of tobacco and the peculiar virtues of many different liquors. He knew birds and beetles and worms; how a weazel would behave in extraordinary circumstances: how to train every breed of horse and dog. He recited goats from the cradle to the grave, could tell the name of any tree from its leaf; knew how a bull could be coerced, a cow cut up, and what plasters were good for a broken head. Sometimes, and often enough, the talk would chance on women, and then he laughed as heartily as anyone else, but he was always relieved when the conversation trailed to more interesting things.

His mother died and left the farm to the younger instead of the elder son; an unusual thing to do, but she did detest him. She knew her younger son very well. He was foreign to her in nothing. His temper ran parallel with her own, his tastes were hers, his ideas had been largely derived from her, she could track them at any time and make or demolish him. He would go to a dance or a picnic and be as exhilarated as she was, and would discuss the matter afterwards. He could speak with some cogency on the shape of this and that female person, the hat of such a one, the disagreeableness of tea at this house and the goodness of it at the other. He could even listen to one speaking without going to sleep at the fourth word. In all he was a decent, quiet lad who would become a father the exact replica of his own, and whose daughters would resemble his mother as closely as two peas resemble their green ancestors—so she left him the farm.

Of course, there was no attempt to turn the elder brother out. Indeed, for some years the two men worked quietly together and prospered and were contented; then, as was inevitable, the younger brother got married, and the elder had to look out for a new place to live in, and to work in—things had become difficult.

It is very easy to say that in such and such circumstances a man should do this and that well-pondered thing, but the courts of logic have as yet the most circumscribed jurisdiction. Just as statistics can prove anything and be quite wrong, so reason can sit in its padded chair issuing pronouncements which are seldom within measurable distance of any reality. Everything is true only in relation to its centre of thought. Some people think with their heads—their subsequent actions are as logical and unpleasant as are those of the other sort who think only with their blood, and this latter has its irrefutable logic also. He thought in this subterranean fashion, and if he had thought in the other the issue would not have been any different.

Still, it was not an easy problem for him, or for any person lacking initiative—a sexual characteristic. He might have emigrated, but his roots were deeply struck in his own place, so the idea never occurred to him; furthermore, our thoughts are often no deeper than our pockets, and one wants money to move anywhere. For any other life than that of farming he had no training and small desire. He had no money and he was a farmer's son. Without money he could not get a farm; being a farmer's son he could not sink to the degradation of a day labourer; logically he could sink, actually he could not without endangering his own centres and verities—so he also got married.

He married a farm of about ten acres, and the sun began to shine on him once more; but only for a few days. Suddenly the sun went away from the heavens; the moon disappeared from the silent night; the silent night itself fled afar, leaving in its stead a noisy, dirty blackness through which one slept or yawned as one could. There was the farm, of course—one could go there and work; but the freshness went out of the very ground; the crops lost their sweetness and candour; the horses and cows disowned him; the goats ceased to be his friends—It was all up with him. He did not whistle any longer. He did not swing his shoulders as he walked, and, although he continued to smoke, he did not look for a particular green bank whereon he could sit quietly flooded with those slow thoughts that had no words.

For he discovered that he had not married a farm at all. He had married a woman—a thin-jawed, elderly slattern, whose sole beauty was her farm. How her jaws worked! The processions and congregations of words that fell and dribbled and slid out of them! Those jaws were never quiet, and in spite of all he did not say anything. There was not anything to say, but much to do from which he shivered away in terror. He looked at her sometimes through the muscles of his arms, through his big, strong hands, through fogs and fumes and singular, quiet tumults that raged within him. She lessoned him on the things he knew so well, and she was always wrong. She lectured him on those things which she did know, but the unending disquisition, the perpetual repetition, the foolish, empty emphasis, the dragging weightiness of her tongue made him repudiate her knowledge and hate it as much as he did her.

Sometimes, looking at her, he would rub his eyes and yawn with fatigue and wonder—There she was! A something enwrapped about with petticoats. Veritably alive. Active as an insect! Palpable to the touch! And what was she doing to him? Why did she do it? Why didn't she go away? Why didn't she die? What sense was there in the making of such a creature that clothed itself like a bolster, without any freedom or entertainment or shapeliness?

Her eyes were fixed on him and they always seemed to be angry; and her tongue was uttering rubbish about horses, rubbish about cows, rubbish about hay and oats. Nor was this the sum of his weariness. It was not alone that he was married; he was multitudinously, egregiously married. He had married a whole family, and what a family.

Her mother lived with her, her eldest sister lived with her, her youngest sister lived with her—and these were all swathed about with petticoats and shawls. They had no movement. Their feet were like those of no creature he had ever observed. One could hear the flip-flap of their slippers all over the place, and at all hours. They were down-at-heel, draggle-tailed, and futile. There was no workmanship about them. They were as unfinished, as unslightly as a puddle on a road. They insulted his eyesight, his hearing, and his energy. They had lank hair that slapped about them like wet seaweed, and they were all talking, talking, talking.

The mother was of an incredible age. She was

senile with age. Her cracked cackle never ceased for an instant. She talked to the dog and the cat; she talked to the walls of the room; she spoke out through the window to the weather; she shut her eyes in a corner and harangued the circumambient darkness. The eldest sister was as silent as a deep ditch and as ugly. She slid here and there with her head on one side like an inquisitive hen watching one curiously, and was always doing nothing with an air of futile employment. The youngest was a semi-lunatic who prattled and prattled without ceasing, and was always catching one's sleeve, and laughing at one's face—and everywhere those flopping, wriggling petticoats were appearing and disappearing. One saw slack hair whisking by the corner of one's eye. Mysteriously, urgently, they were coming and going and coming again, and never, never being silent.

More and more he went running to the public-house. But it was no longer to be among men, it was to get drunk. One might imagine him sitting there thinking those slow thoughts without words. One might predict that the day would come when he would realise very suddenly, very clearly, all that he had been thinking about, and, when this urgent, terrible thought had been translated into its own terms of action, he would be quietly hanged by the neck until he was as dead as he had been before he was alive.

Desire

I

He was excited, and as he leaned forward in his chair and told this story to his wife he revealed to her a degree or a species of credulity of which she could not have believed him capable.

He was a level-headed man, and habitually conducted his affairs on hard-headed principles. He had conducted his courtship, his matrimonial and domestic affairs in a manner which she should not have termed reckless or romantic. When, therefore, she found him excited, and over such a story, she did not know how just to take the matter.

She compromised by agreeing with him, not because her reason was satisfied or even touched, but simply because he was excited, and a woman can welcome anything which varies the dull round and will bathe in exclamations if she gets the chance.

This was what he told her.

As he was walking to lunch a motor car came down the street at a speed much too dangerous for the narrow and congested thoroughfare. A man was walking in front of him, and, just as the car came behind, this man stepped off the path with a view to crossing the road. He did not even look behind as he stepped off. Her husband stretched a ready arm that swept the man back to the pavement one second before the car went blaring and buzzing by.

'If I had not been there,' said her husband, who liked slang, 'you would have got it where the chicken got the axe.'

The two men grinned at each other; her husband smiling with good-fellowship, the other crinkling with amusement and gratitude.

They walked down the street and, on the strength of that adventure, they had lunch together.

They had sat for a long time after lunch, making each other's acquaintance, smoking innumerable cigarettes, and engaged in a conversation which she could never have believed her husband would have shared in for ten minutes; and they had parted with a wish, from her husband, that they should meet again on the following day, and a wordless smile from the man.

He had neither ratified nor negatived the arrangement.

'I hope he'll turn up,' said her husband.

This conversation had excited her man, for it had drawn him into an atmosphere to which he was a stranger, and he had found himself moving there with such pleasure that he wished to get back to it with as little delay as possible.

Briefly, as he explained it to her, the atmosphere was religious; and while it was entirely intellectual it was more heady and exhilarating than the emotional religion to which he had been accustomed, and from which he had silently lapsed.

He tried to describe his companion; but had such ill success in the description that she could not remember afterwards whether he was tall or short; fat or thin; fair or dark.

It was the man's eyes only that he succeeded in emphasising; and these, it appeared, were eyes such as he had never before seen in a human face.

That also, he amended, was a wrong way of putting it, for his eyes were exactly like everybody else's. It was the way he looked through them that was different. Something, very steady, very ardent, very quiet and powerful, was using these eyes for purposes of vision. He had never met anyone who looked at him so comprehendingly; so agreeably.

'You are in love,' said she with a laugh.

After this her husband's explanations became more explanatory but not less confused, until she found that they were both, with curious unconsciousness, in the middle of a fairy-tale.

'He asked me,' said her husband, 'what was the thing I wished for beyond all things.

'That was the most difficult question I have ever been invited to answer,' he went on; 'and for nearly half an hour we sat thinking it out, and discussing magnificences and possibilities.'

'I had all the usual thoughts; and, of course, the first of them was wealth. We are more dominated by proverbial phrases than we conceive of, and, such a question being posed, the words "healthy, wealthy, and wise" will come, unbidden, to answer it. To be alive is to be acquisitive, and so I mentioned wealth, tentatively, as a possibility; and he agreed that it was worth considering. But after a while I knew that I did not want money.'

'One always has need of money,' said his wife.

'In a way, that is true,' he replied, 'but not in this way; for, as I thought it over, I remembered, that we have no children; and that our relatively few desires, or fancies, can be readily satisfied by the money we already have. Also we are fairly well off; we have enough in the stocking to last our time even if I ceased from business, which I am not going to do; and, in short, I discovered that money or its purchasing power had not any particular advantages to offer.'

'All the same!' she murmured; and halted with her eyes fixed on purchasings far away in time and space.

'All the same!' he agreed with a smile.

'I could not think of anything worth wishing for,' he continued. 'I mentioned health and wisdom, and we considered these; but, judging myself by the standard of the world in which we move, I concluded that both my health and knowledge were as good as the next man's; and I thought also that if I elected to become wiser than my contemporaries I might be a very lonely person for the rest of my days.'

'Yes,' said she thoughtfully, 'I am glad you did not ask to be made wise, unless you could have asked it for both of us.'

'I asked him in the end what he would advise me to demand, but he replied that he could not advise me at all. "Behind everything stands desire," said he, "and you must find out your desire."'

'I asked him then, if the conditions were reversed and if the opportunity had come to him instead of to me, what he should have asked for; not, as I explained to him, in order that I might copy his wish, but from sheer curiosity. He replied that he should not ask for anything. This reply astonished, almost alarmed me at first, but most curiously satisfied me on considering it, and I was about to adopt that attitude—'

'Oh,' said his wife.

'When an idea came to me. 'Here I am,' I said to myself, 'forty-eight years of age: rich enough; sound enough in wind and limb; and as wise as I can afford to be. What is there now belonging to me, absolutely mine, but from which I must part, and which I should like to keep?' And I saw that the thing which was leaving me day by day; second by second; irretrievably and inevitably; was my forty-eighth year. I thought I should like to continue at the age of forty-eight until my time was up.'

'I did not ask to live for ever, or any of that nonsense, for I saw that to live for ever is to be condemned to a misery of boredom more dreadful than anything else the mind can conceive of. But, while I do live, I wish to live competently, and so I asked to be allowed stay at the age of forty-eight years with all the equipment of my present state unimpaired.'

'You should not have asked for such a thing,' said his wife, a little angrily. 'It is not fair to me,' she explained. 'You are older than I am now, but in a few years this will mean that I shall be needlessly older than you. I think it was not a loyal wish.'

'I thought of that objection,' said he, 'and I also

114

thought that I was past the age at which certain things matter; and that both temperamentally and in the matter of years I am proof against sensual or such-like attractions. It seemed to me to be right; so I just registered my wish with him.'

'What did he say?' she queried.

'He did not say anything; he just nodded; and began to talk again of other matters—religion, life, death, mind; a host of things, which, for all the diversity they seem to have when I enumerate them, were yet one single theme.'

'I feel a more contented man to-night than I have ever felt,' he continued, 'and I feel in some curious way a different person from the man I was yesterday.'

Here his wife awakened from the conversation and began to laugh.

'You are a foolish man,' said she, 'and I am just as bad. If anyone were to hear us talking this solemn silliness they would have a right to mock at us.'

He laughed heartily with her, and after a light supper they went to bed.

II

During the night his wife had a dream.

She dreamed that a ship set away from the Polar Seas on an expedition in which she was not sufficiently interested to find out its reason. The ship departed with her on board. All that she knew or cared was that she was greatly concerned with baggage, and with counting and going over the various articles that she had brought against Arctic weather.

115

She had thick woollen stockings. She had skin boots all hairy inside, all pliable and wrinkled without. She had a great skin cap shaped like a helmet and fitting down in a cape over her shoulders. She had, and they did not astonish her, a pair of very baggy fur trousers. She had a sleeping sack.

She had an enormous quantity of things; and everybody in the expedition was equipped, if not with the same things, at least similarly.

These traps were a continuous subject of conversation aboard, and, although days and weeks passed, the talk of the ship hovered about and fell continually into the subject of warm clothing.

There came a day when the weather was perceptibly colder; so cold that she was tempted to draw on these wonderful breeches, and to fit her head into that most comfortable hat. But she did not do so; for, and everybody on the ship explained it to her, it was necessary that she should accustom herself to the feeling, the experience, of cold; and, she was further assured, that the chill which she was now resenting was nothing to the freezing she should presently have to bear.

It seemed good advice; and she decided that as long as she could bear the cold she would do so, and would not put on any protective covering; thus, when the cold became really intense, she would be in some measure inured to it, and would not suffer so much.

But steadily, and day by day, the weather grew colder.

For now they were in wild and whirling seas wherein great green and white icebergs went sailing by; and all about the ship little hummocks of ice bobbed and surged, and went under and came up; and the grey water slashed and hissed against and on top of these small hillocks.

Her hands were so cold that she had to put them under her armpits to keep any warmth in them; and her feet were in a worse condition. They had begun to pain her; so she decided that on the morrow she would put on her winter equipment, and would not mind what anybody said to the contrary.

'It is cold enough,' said she 'for my Arctic trousers, for my warm soft boots, and my great furry gloves. I will put them on in the morning,' for it was then almost night and she meant to go to bed at once.

She did go to bed; and she lay there in a very misery of cold.

In the morning, she was yet colder; and immediately on rising she looked for the winter clothing which she had laid ready by the side of her bunk the night before; but she could not find them. She was forced to dress in her usual rather thin clothes; and, having done so, she went on deck.

When she got to the side of the vessel she found that the world about her had changed.

The sea had disappeared. Far as the eye could peer was a level plain of ice, not white, but dull grey; and over it there lowered a sky, grey as itself and of almost the same dullness.

Across this waste there blew a bitter, a piercing wind that her eyes winced from, and that caused her ears to tingle and sting.

Not a soul was moving on the ship, and the dead silence which brooded on the ice lay heavy and almost solid on the vessel.

She ran to the other side, and found that the whole ship's company had landed, and were staring at her from a little distance off the ship. And these people were as silent as the frozen air, as the frozen ship. They stared at her; they made no move; they made no sound.

She noticed that they were all dressed in their winter furs; and, while she stood, ice began to creep into her veins.

One of the ship's company strode forward a few paces and held up a bundle in his mittened hand. She was amazed to see that the bundle contained her clothes; her broad furry trousers; her great cosy helmet and gloves.

To get from the ship to the ice was painful but not impossible. A rope ladder was hanging against the side, and she went down this. The rungs felt hard as iron, for they were frozen stiff; and the touch of those glassy surfaces bit into her tender hand like fire. But she got to the ice and went across it towards her companions.

Then, to her dismay, to her terror, all these, suddenly, with one unexpressed accord, turned and began to run away from her; and she, with a heart that shook once and could scarcely beat again, took after them.

Every few paces she fell, for her shoes could not grip on the ice; and each time that she fell those monsters stood and turned and watched her, and the man who had her clothes waved the bundle at her and danced grotesquely, silently.

She continued running, sliding, falling, picking herself up, until her breath went, and she came to a halt, unable to move a limb further and scarcely able to breathe; and this time they did not stay to look at her.

They continued running, but now with great and greater speed, with the very speed of madmen; and she saw them become black specks away on the white distance; and she saw them disappear; and she saw that there was nothing where she stared but the long white miles, and the terrible silence, and the cold.

How cold it was!

And with that there arose a noiseless wind, keen as a razor.

It stung into her face; it swirled about her ankles like a lash; it stabbed under her armpits like a dagger.

'I am cold,' she murmured.

She looked backwards whence she had come, but the ship was no longer in sight, and she could not remember from what direction she had come.

Then she began to run in any direction.

Indeed she ran in every direction to find the ship; for when she had taken a hundred steps in one way she thought, frantically, 'this is not the way,' and at once she began to run on the opposite road. But run as she might she could not get warm; it was colder she got. And then, on a steel-grey plane, she slipped, and slipped again, and went sliding down a hollow, faster and faster; she came to the brink of a cleft, and swished over this, and down into a hole of ice and there she lay.

'I shall die!' she said. 'I shall fall asleep here and die. . . . '

Then she awakened.

She opened her eyes directly on the window and

saw the ghost of dawn struggling with the ghoul of darkness. A greyish perceptibility framed the window without, but could not daunt the obscurity within; and she lay for a moment terrified at that grotesque adventure, and thanking God that it had only been a dream.

In another second she felt that she was cold. She pulled the clothes more tightly about her, and she spoke to her husband.

'How miserably cold it is!' she said.

She turned in the bed and snuggled against him for warmth; and she found that an atrocity of cold came from him; that he was icy.

She leaped from the bed with a scream. She switched on the light, and bent over her husband.

He was stone dead. He was stone cold. And she stood by him, shivering and whimpering.

Hunger

I

On some people misery comes unrelentingly. It comes with such a continuous rage that one might say destruction had been sworn against them and that they were doomed beyond appeal, or hope.

That seemed to her to be the case as she sat, when her visitor had departed, looking on life as it had moved about her; and she saw that life had closed on her, had crushed her, and that there was nothing to be said about it, and no one to be blamed.

She was ten years married, and she had three children. One of them had fallen when he was a baby, and had hurt his back so badly that the dispensary doctor instructed her not to let him walk for a few years.

She loved all her children, but this child she loved greatly; for she had to do more for him than for the others. Indeed she had to do everything for him, and she did not grudge doing it. He was the eldest and he was always with her. The other youngsters were with her as screamings, as demands, to be attended to and forgotten, but he was with her as a companion eye, a consciousness to whom she could talk and who would reply to her, and who would not, could not, by any means get into mischief.

Her husband was a house-painter, and when work was brisk he got good wages: he could earn thirty-five shillings a week when he was working.

But his work was constant only in the summer months: through the bad weather there was no call for him, for no one wanted house-painting done in the winter; and so the money which he earned in the fine months had to be stretched and made to cover the dead months.

Nor were these five months to be entirely depended upon: here and there in a week days would be missed, and with that his Society dues had to be paid, for he would pay these though he starved for it.

II

Wages which have to be stretched so lengthily give but the slenderest sum towards a weekly budget. It was she who had to stretch them, and the doing of it occupied all the time she could spare for thinking.

She made ends meet where nothing was but ends, and they met just over the starvation line.

She had not known for years what it was like not to be hungry for one day; but life is largely custom; and neither she nor her husband nor the children made much complaint about a condition which was normal for them all, and into which the children had been born.

They could scarcely die of hunger for they were native to it. They were hunger. There was no other hunger but them: and they only made a noise about food when they saw food.

If she could have got work how gladly she would have taken it! How gladly she would have done it! Sweated work! Any work! so it brought in if it was no more than a few coppers in the day. But the children were there, three of them, and all were young and one was a cripple.

Her own people, and those of her husband, lived, existed, far away in the country. They could not take the children off her hands. She could not give a neighbour anything to look after them while she went out working. She was held to them as fast as if she were chained to them; and, for to think in such cases is only to be worried, there was no use in thinking about it. She had already all the worry she could deal with, and she wanted no more.

She remembered a tale that she had laughed at, when she was young, about a woman who had been circumstanced as she was now. This woman used to put her two children into a box, for she had to go out every day to work in order that she might feed them; and she kept them in the box so that they might not injure themselves during her absence.

It was a good idea, but the children came out of the box hunchbacks, and so stunted in their growth that it might be said they never grew thereafter. It might have been better for the children, and easier for them, if they had died; anyhow, their mother died, and the poor little oddities went to the workhouse; and must all their lives have got all the jeers which their appearance sanctioned.

There was nothing to be done; even her husband had long ago given up thinking of how this could be arranged; and although she still, and continually, thought about it, she knew that nothing could be done.

III

Her husband was a jolly man; he used to make up lists of the gigantic feeds they would have when the ship came home (what ship he did not say, nor was it understood that he expected one), and he or she or the children would remind each other of foods which had been left out of his catalogue; for no food of which they knew the name could justly be omitted from their future.

He was a robust man, and could have eaten a lot had he got it. Indeed he had often tempted his wife to commit an act of madness and have one wild blow-out; for which, as she pointed out to him, they would have to pay by whole days of whole starvation, instead of the whole days of semi-hunger to which they were accustomed.

This was the only subject on which they came nigh to quarrelling, and he brought it forward with fortnightly regularity.

Sometimes she went cold at the thought that on some pay-day he might go in for a wild orgy of eating, and perhaps spend half a crown. Less than that sum could not nearly fill him; and the double of it would hardly fill him the way he needed to be filled; for he wanted to be filled as tightly as a drum, and with such a weight and abundance of victual that he could scarcely be lifted by a crane.

But he was an honourable man, and she knew that he would not do this unless she and the children were with him and could share and go mad with him. He was very fond of them, and if she could have fed him on her own flesh she would have sacrificed a slice or two, for she was very fond of him.

IV

The mild weather had come, and he got a cut in his hand, which festered and seemed stubbornly incurable. The reason was that the gaunt man was not fed well enough to send clean blood down to doctor his cut hand. In the end he did get over it; but for three weeks he had been unable to work, for who will give employment to a man whose hand looks like a poultice or a small football?

The loss of these three weeks almost finished her.

The distinguishing mark of her family had been thinness, it was now bonyness.

To what a food-getting fervour was she compelled! She put the world of rubbish that was about her through a sieve; and winnowed nourishment for her family where a rat would have unearthed disappointment.

She could not beg; but she did send her two children into the street, and sometimes one of these got a copper from a passing stranger. Then, like the call of a famished crow who warns his brothers that he has discovered booty, that youngster gave out a loyal squeal for his companion; and they trotted home with their penny. The sun shone on the day they got a penny; on the days when they got nothing the sun might bubble the tar and split the bricks, but it did not shine.

Her man returned to his work, and if she could hold on they would be able to regain the poverty of a few months previously, but which now beamed to her as distant, unattainable affluence.

She could hold on, and she did; so that they tided feebly across those evil days; and came nigh at last to the longed-for scarcity which yet was not absolute starvation; and whereby they could live in the condition of health to which they were accustomed, and which they recognised and spoke of as good health.

They could not absolutely come to this for at least a year. Provision had still to be made for the lean months to come; the winter months; and more than three weeks' wages which should have been skimmed in this precaution had been unprofitable, had not existed. The difference had to be made up by a double skimming of the present wage; which must also pay the present necessities, and recoup the baker and grocer for the few weeks' credit these shop people had given her.

In all, their lot for a long time was not to be envied, except by a beast in captivity: and envied only by him because he lusts for freedom and the chance of it as we lust for security and the destruction of chance.

V

The winter came—the winter will come though the

lark protest and the worm cries out its woe—and she entered on that period with misgiving, with resolution, and with a facing of everything that might come.

What bravery she had! What a noble, unwearying courage; when in so little a time, and at so small a pain, she might have died!

But such an idea did not come to her head. She looked on the world, and she saw that it was composed of a man and three children; while they lasted she could last, and when they were done it would be time enough to think of personal matters and her relation to things.

Before the summer had quite ended, e'er autumn had tinted a leaf, the war broke out; and with its coming there came insecurity. Not to her, not to them. They had no standard to measure security by. It came to the people who desire things done, and who pay to have doors varnished or window-frames painted. These people drew silently but resolutely from expense; while he and she and the children sunk deeper into their spending as one wallows into a bog.

The prices of things began to increase with a cumulative rapidity, and the quality of things began to deteriorate with equal speed. Bread and the eater of it came to a grey complexion. Meat was no more. The vegetables emigrated with the birds. The potato got a rise in the world and recognised no more its oldest friends. Nothing was left but the rain; and the rain came loyally.

They, those others, could retrench and draw in a little their horns; but from what could she retreat? What could she avoid? What could she eliminate, who had come to the bare bone and shank of life? The necessity for the loaf comes daily, recurs pitilessly from digestion to digestion, and with the inexorable promptitude of the moon the rent collector wanes and waxes.

They managed.

She and he managed.

Work still was, although it was spaced and intervalled like a storm-blown hedge. Here was a week and there another one, and from it they gleaned their constricted existence.

They did not complain; for those who are down do not complain. Nor did they know they were down. Or, knowing it, they did not admit their downness. For to front so final a fact is to face with naked hands a lion; and to admit is to give in. Is to be washed away. To be lost and drowned. To be anonymous; unhelpable; alive no more; but debris, or a straw which the wind takes and sails, or tears, or drifts, or rots, to powder and forgetfulness.

A bone in the world of bones! And they gnawed these bones until it seemed that nothing moved in the world except their teeth.

VI

The winter came, and his work stopped as it always did in that season.

He got jobs cleaning windows. He got jobs at the docks hoisting things which not Hercules nor the devil himself could lift. But which he could lift, or which his teeth and the teeth of his children detached from the ground as from foundations and rivettings.

He got a job as a coalman; and as a night-watch-man sitting in the angle of a black street before a bucket of stinking coal, which had been a fire until the rain put it out. To-day he had a job; but to-morrow and for a week he had none.

With what had been saved, skimmed, strained from the summer wages; with what came from the jobs; with the pennies that the children unearthed from strangers as though they dug in those loath souls for coin, they lived through the winter, and did not feel that they had passed through an experience worthy of record, or that their endurance might have been rewarded with medals and a pension.

They were living, as we all manage, amazingly, to live: and if others had an easier time that was their chance. But this was their life, and there were those who were even worse off than they were.

For they paid the rent! And, when that was done, what a deed had been accomplished! How notable an enemy circumvented!

VII

The spring came; but it brought no leaves to their tree. The summer came; but it did not come to them; nor warn them of harvest and a sickle in the yield.

There was no building done that summer; the price of material had gone up and the price of wages. The contractors did not care for that prospect, and the client, remembering taxes and the war, decided to wait.

And her husband had no work!

Almost he had even given up looking for work. He would go out of the house and come into the house and go out of the house again; and he and she would look at each other in a dumb questioning.

It was strange how he had arranged with himself not to look at the children. How he had even arranged that their whimperings should seem to be inaudible, and their very presences invisable! And they, having raked his coming as with search-lights, and discovering that he brought nothing, looked at him no more.

They looked at her. They projected themselves to her, about her, upon her, into her. . . .

A wolf-mother, thus badgered and possessed, would have escaped from her young by mercifully or unmercifully slaughtering them. But she still could preserve her soul, her tenderness. Yet, if a whole infinity of tenderness seemed to be preserved for the children, a major, a yet more marvellous, tenderness was reserved for her man—it was without words, without action. It was without anything whatever. It was itself alone. Unproven, unquestioned, unending. To be perceived, received, only by the soul, and from the soul, or not to be received or perceived at all.

Sometimes she would say—not that she had anything to say, but to ease her husband's heart with a comradely word—

'Any chance to-day, do you think?'

And he would reply:

'Chance!'

And he would sit down to brood upon that lapsing word.

They were not angry; they had not the blood to

130

be angry with; for to be wrathful you must be well fed or you must be drunk.

The youngest child died of an ill which, whatever it was at the top, was hunger at the bottom; and she grew terrified. She heard that there was work to be had in the Munition Factories in Scotland, and by some means she gathered together the fare and sent her husband across the sea.

'Write, if you can,' said she, 'the minute you get a place.'

'Yes,' he replied.

'And send us what you can spare,' she said. 'Send something this week if you can.'

'Yes,' he said.

And he went away.

And she went into the streets to beg.

VIII

She left the boy behind in his chair, and brought the other little one with her.

She was frightened, for one can be arrested for begging. And she was afraid not to beg, for one can die of hunger.

How well she knew those streets! and yet she did not know them in this aspect! These were atrocious streets!

She got a penny here and a penny there, and she bought bread. Sometimes even she bought a twist of tea. She could manage until the end of the week; until her man sent the money.

She had thoughts of singing at the corners of streets, as she had so often seen done by the tone-less, ashen-faced women, who creak rusty music at the passer, and fix him with their eyes. But she was ashamed; and no song that she could remember seemed suitable; and she only could remember bits of songs; and she knew that her voice would not work for her, but that it would creak and mourn like a rusty hinge.

Her earnings were small, for she could not get in touch with people. That too is a trade and must be learned. They recognised her at a distance as a beggar, and she could only whisper to the back of a head or a cold shoulder.

Sometimes when she went towards a person that person instantly crossed the road and walked for a while hastily.

Sometimes people fixed upon her a prohibitive eye and she drew back from them humbled; her heart panting and her eyes hot at the idea that they took her for a beggar.

At times a man, without glancing at her, stuck a hand in a pocket and gave her a penny without halting in his stride.

One day she got twopence; one day she got sixpence; one day she got nothing.

But she could hold out to the end of the week.

IX

The end of the week came, but it brought no letter.

'It will come to-morrow,' she said.

'He is in a strange country,' she thought in panic. 'He must have missed the post, God help him!'

But on the next day there was no letter; nor any letter on the day after; and on the day that succeeded to it there was no letter.

'He . . .!' she said.

But she could not speculate on him. She knew him too well, and she knew that this was not he; he could no more leave them in the lurch than he could jump across Ireland in one jump.

'He has not got work,' she said.

And she saw him strayed and stranded; without a hand; without a voice; bewildered and lost among strangers; going up streets and down streets; and twisting himself into a maze, a dizziness of loneliness and hunger and despair.

Or, she said:

'The submarines had blown up the ship that was coming with the money.'

The week went by; another came, and still she did not hear from him. She was not able to pay the rent.

She looked at the children; and then she looked away from them distantly to her strayed husband; and then she looked inwardly on herself, and there was nothing to see.

She was down.

No littlest hope could find a chink to peer through. And while she sat, staring at nothing, in an immobile maze of attention, her mind—she had no longer a heart, it had died of starvation—her mind would give a leap and be still; and would leap again, as though an unknown, wordless action were seeking to be free; seeking to do something; seeking to disprove stagnation, and powerlessness, and death; and a little burning centre of violence hung in her head like a star.

She followed people with her eyes, sometimes a little way with her feet, saying to herself:

'The pockets of that man are full of money; he would rattle if he fell.'

Or:

'That man had his breakfast this morning; he is full of food to the chin; he is round and tight and solid, and he weighs a ton.'

She said:

'If I had all the money of all the people in this street I should have a lot of money.'

She said:

'If I owned all the houses in this street I should have a lot of money.'

The rent collector told her imperatively that she must leave at the end of the week, and the children called to her for bread, clamorously, unceasingly, like little dogs that yap and whine and cannot be made to stop.

X

Relief kitchens had been started in various parts of the city, but she only heard of them by chance; and she went to one. She told a lady in attendance her miserable tale, and was given the address of a gentleman who might assist her. He could give her a ticket which would enable her to get food; and he might be able to set her in the way of earning what would pay the rent.

This lady thought her husband had deserted her; and she said so, without condemnation, as one states a thing which has been known to happen; and the poor woman agreed without agreeing, for she did

134

not believe it.

But she did not argue about the matter, for now that she accepted food, she accepted anything that came with it, whether it was opinions or advice. She was an acceptor, and if she claimed to possess even an opinion it might jeopardise her chance of getting anything.

She set out for the house of the gentleman who could give her the ticket which would get her food to bring home to the children.

He lived at some distance, and when she got to his house the servant told her he had gone to his office; at his office she was informed that he had gone out. She called three times at the office, and on the third time she was told that he had come in, but had gone home.

She trudged to his house again; and would have been weary, but that her mind had lapsed far, far, from her trudging feet; and when the mind is away the body matters nothing.

Where was her mind? At times it was nowhere. It was gone from her body and from material things. It might be said to have utterly quitted that tenement, and to be somehow, somewhere, refuged from every fear, havened from every torment and eased of every memory that could deject it. She was life and a will; or, if these are but one, she was the will to be, obscure, diligent, indefatigable.

And then, again, as at the opening of a door, her mind, laden with recollections of time and space, of deeds and things and thwartings, was back in the known and incredible room, looking at the children, listening to them, consoling them; telling them that in a little while she should be home again, and that she would bring them food.

They had not eaten anything for—how long was it? Was it a year? Had they ever eaten? And one of them was sick!

She must get back. She had been away too long. But she must go forward before she could go back.

She must get the ticket which was food and hope and a new beginning, or a respite. Then she should be able to look about her. The children would go to sleep; and she could plan and contrive and pull together those separated and dwindling ends.

She came to the gentleman's house. He was in, and she told him her story, and how her case was desperate.

He also believed that her husband had deserted her; and he promised to write by that night's post to find out the truth about the man, and to see that he was punished for his desertion.

He had no tickets with him; he had used them all, for the hungry people in Dublin were numerous: work was slack everywhere, and those who had never before applied for assistance were now obliged to do so by dreadful necessity. He gave her some money, and promised to call at her room on the following day to investigate her case.

She went homewards urgently, and near home she bought bread and tea.

When she got in the crippled boy turned dull, dumb eyes upon her; and she laughed at him excitedly, exultantly; for she had food; lots of it, two loaves of it.

But the other child did not turn to her, and would not turn to her again, for he was dead; and he was dead of hunger.

XI

She could not afford to go mad, for she still had a boy and he depended on her with an utter helpless dependence.

She fed him and fed herself; running from him in the chair to that other in its cot, with the dumb agony of an animal who must do two things at once, and cannot resolve which thing to do.

She could not think; she could hardly feel. She was dulled and distressed and wild. She was weakened by misery and tormented by duties; and life and the world seemed a place of busynesses, and futilities, and unending, unregulated, demands upon her.

A neighbour, hearing that persistent trotting over her head, came up to the room to remonstrate, and remained to shed for her the tears which she could not weep herself. She, too, was in straits, and had nothing more to give than those tears; and the banal iterations which are comfort because they are kindness.

Into this place the gentleman called on the following day to investigate, and was introduced to a room swept almost as clean of furniture as a dog kennel is; to the staring, wise-eyed child who lived in a chair; and to the quiet morsel of death that lay in a cot by the wall.

He was horrified, but he was used to sights of misery; and he knew that when things have ceased to move they must be set moving again; and that all he could do was to remove some of the impediments which he found in the path of life, so that it might flow on before it had time to become stagnant and rotten.

He took from the dry-eyed, tongue-tied woman all the immediate worry of death. He paid the rent, and left something to go on with as well; and he promised to get her work either in his house or at his office, but he would get her work to do somehow.

XII

He came daily; and each day, in reply to her timid question as to her husband, he had nothing to say except that enquiries were being made.

On the fifth day he had news, and he would have preferred any duty, however painful, to the duty of telling her his news.

But he told it, sitting on the one chair; with his hand over his eyes, and nothing of his face visible except the mouth which shaped and spoke sentences.

The munition people in Scotland reported that a man of the name he was enquiring for had applied for work, and had been taken on a fortnight after his application. The morning after he began work he was found dead in a laneway. He had no lodgings in the city; and at the post-mortem examination it was found that he had died of hunger and exposure.

She listened to that tale; looking from the gentleman who told it to her little son who listened to it. She moistened her lips with her tongue; but she could not speak, she could only stammer and smile.

The gentleman also sat looking at the boy.

'We must set this young man up,' said he heavily. 'I shall send a doctor to look him over to-day.'

And he went away all hot and cold; beating his hands together as he walked; and feeling upon his shoulders all the weariness and misery of the world.

Schoolfellows

We had been at school together and I remembered
him perfectly well, for he had been a clever and
prominent boy. He won prizes for being at the top
of his class; and prizes for good behaviour; and
prizes for games. Whatever prizes were going we
knew that he should get them; and, although he was
pleasant about it, he knew it himself.

He saw me first, and he shouted and waved his
hat, but I had jumped on a tram already in motion.
He ran after me for quite a distance; but the trams
only stop at regular places, and he could not keep
up: he fell behind, and was soon left far behind.

I had intended jumping off to shake his hand;
but I thought, so fast did he run, that he would
catch up; and then the tram went quicker and
quicker; and quite a stream of cars and taxis were in
the way; so that when the tram did stop he was out
of sight. Also I was in a hurry to get home.

Going home I marvelled for a few moments that

he should have run so hard after me. He ran almost—desperately.

'It would strain every ounce of a man's strength to run like that!' I said.

And his eyes had glared as he ran!

'Poor old chap!' I thought. 'He must have wanted to speak to me very badly.'

Three or four days afterwards I met him again; and we talked together for a while on the footpath. Then, at whose suggestion I do not remember, we moved into the bar of an hotel near by.

We drank several glasses of something; for which, noticing that his hat was crumpled and his coat sleeves shiny, I paid. We spoke of the old days at school and he told me of men whom he had met, but whom I had not heard of for a long time. Such old schoolfellows as I did know of I mentioned, and in every instance he took their addresses down on a piece of paper.

He asked what I was doing and how I was succeeding and where I lived; and this latter information he pencilled also on his piece of paper.

'My memory is getting bad,' he said with a smile.

Every few minutes he murmured into our school-day conversation—

'Whew! Isn't it hot!'

And at other times, laughing a little, apologising a little, he said:

'I am terribly thirsty to-day; it's the heat I suppose.'

I had not noticed that it was particularly hot; but we are as different in our skins as we are in our souls, and one man's heat may be tepid enough to his neighbour.

II

Then I met him frequently. One goes home usually at the same hour and by the same road; and it was on these home-goings and on this beaten track that we met.

Somehow, but by what subtle machinery I cannot recall, we always elbowed one another into a bar; and, as his hat was not getting less crumpled nor his coat less shiny, I paid for whatever liquor was consumed.

One can do anything for a long time without noticing it, and the paying for a few drinks is not likely to weigh on the memory. Still, we end by noticing everything; and perhaps I noticed it the earlier because liquor does not agree with me. I never mentioned that fact to anyone, being slightly ashamed of it, but I knew it very woefully myself by the indigestion which for two or three days followed on even a modest consumption of alcohol.

So it was that setting homeward one evening on the habitual track I turned very deliberately from it; and, with the slightest feeling of irritation, I went homewards by another route: and each night that followed I took this new path.

I did not see him for some weeks, and then one evening he hailed me on the new road. When I turned at the call and saw him running—he was running—I was annoyed, and, as we shook hands, I became aware that it was not so much the liquor I was trying to side-track as my old schoolfellow.

He walked with me for quite a distance; and he

talked more volubly than was his wont. He talked excitedly; and his eyes searched the streets ahead as they widened out before our steps, or as they were instantly and largely visible when we turned a corner. A certain malicious feeling was in my mind as we paced together; I thought:

'There is no public-house on this road.'

Before we parted he borrowed a half-sovereign from me saying that he would pay it back in a day or two, but I cheerfully bade adieu to the coin as I handed it over, and thought also that I was bidding a lengthy adieu to him.

'I won't meet him for quite a while,' I said to myself; and that proved to be true.

III

Nevertheless when a fair month had elapsed I did meet him again, and we marched together in a silence which was but sparsely interrupted by speech.

He had apparently prospected my new route, for he informed me that a certain midway side-street was a short cut; and midway in this side-street we found a public-house.

I went into this public-house with the equable pulse of a man who has no true grievance; for, I should have been able to provide against a contingency which even the worst equipped prophet might have predicted.

As often as his glass was emptied I saw that it was refilled; but, and perhaps with a certain ostentation, I refrained myself from the cup.

Of course, one drink leads to another, and the path between each is conversational. My duty it appeared was to supply the drinks, but I thought it just that he should supply the conversation.

I had myself a fund of silence which might have been uncomfortable to a different companion, and against which he was forced to deploy many verbal battalions.

We had now met quite a number of times. He had exhausted our schooldays as a topic; he knew nothing about politics or literature or city scandal, and talk about weather dies of inanition in less than a minute; and yet—he may have groaned at the necessity—there had to be fashioned a conversational bridge which should unite drink to drink, or drinks must cease.

In such a case a man will talk about himself. It is one's last subject; but it is a subject upon which, given the preliminary push, one may wax eternally eloquent.

He rehearsed to me a serial tale of unmerited calamity, and of hardship by field and flood; of woes against which he had been unable to provide, and against which no man could battle; and of accidents so attuned to the chords of fiction that one knew they had to be true. He had been to rustic-sounding places in England and to Spanish-sounding places in America; and from each of these places an undefined but complete misfortune had uprooted him and chased him as with a stick. So by devious, circuitous, unbelievable routes he had come home again.

One cannot be utterly silent unless one is dead, and then possibly one makes a crackle with one's bones; so I spoke:

'You are glad to be home again,' I queried.

He was glad; but he was glad dubiously and with reservations. Misfortune had his address, and here or elsewhere could thump a hand upon his shoulder.

His people were not treating him decently, it appeared. They had been content to see him return from outlandish latitudes, but since then they had not given him a fair show.

Domestic goblins hinted at, not spoken, but which one sensed to be grisly, half detached themselves from between the drinks. He was not staying with his people. They made him an allowance. You could not call it an allowance either: they paid him a weekly sum. Weekly sum was a large way of putting it, for you cannot do much on fifteen shillings a week: that sum per week would hardly pay for, for—

'The drinks,' I put in brightly; for one cannot be persistently morose in jovial company.

'I must be off,' I said, and I filled the chink of silence which followed on my remark with a waving hand and the bustle of my hasty departure.

IV

Two evenings afterwards he met me again.

We did not shake hands; and my salutation was so brief as not really to merit that name.

He fell in beside me and made a number of remarks about the weather; which, if they were as difficult to make as they were to listen to, must have been exceedingly troublesome to him. One saw him searching as in bottomless pits for something to say; and he hauled a verbal wisp from these profunderies with the labour of one who drags miseries up a mountain.

The man was pitiable, and I pitied him. I went alternately hot and cold. I blushed for him and for myself; for the stones under our feet and for the light clouds that went scudding above our heads; and in another instant I was pale with rage at his shameful, shameless persistence. I thrust my hands into my pockets, because they were no longer hands but fists; and because they tingled and were inclined to jerk without authority from me.

We came to the midway, cross-street which as well as being a short cut was the avenue to a public-house; and he dragged slightly at the crossing as I held to my course.

'This is the longest way,' he murmured.

'I prefer it,' I replied.

After a moment he said:

'You always go home this way.'

'I shall go a different way to-morrow,' I replied.

'What way?' he enquired timidly.

'I must think that out,' said I.

With that I stood and resolutely bade him good-bye. We both moved a pace from each other, and then he turned again, flurriedly, and asked me for the loan of a half a crown.

He wanted it to get a—a—a—

I gave it to him hurriedly and walked away, prickling with a sensation of weariness and excitement as of one who has been worried by a dog but has managed to get away from it.

Then I did not see him for two days, but of course I knew that I should meet him, and the knowledge was as exasperating as any kind of

146

knowledge could be.

V

It was quite early in the morning; and he was waiting outside my house. He accompanied me to the tram, and on the way asked me for a half a crown. I did not give it, and I did not reply to him.

As I was getting on the tram he lowered his demand and asked me urgently for sixpence. I did not answer nor look at him, but got on my tram and rode away in such a condition of nervous fury that I could have assaulted the conductor who asked me to pay my fare.

When I reached home that evening he was still waiting for me; at least, he was there, and he may have hung about all day; or he may have arrived just in time to catch me.

At the sight of him all the irritation which had almost insensibly been adding to and multiplying and storing itself in my mind, fused together into one sole consciousness of rage which not even a language of curses could make explicit enough to suit my need of expression. I swore when I saw him; and I cursed him openly when he came to me with the sly, timid, outfacing bearing, which had become for me his bearing.

He began at once; for all pretence was gone, and all the barriers of reserve and decency were down. He did not care what I thought of him: nor did he heed in the least what I said to him. He did not care about anything except only by an means; by every means; by cajolery, or savagery, or sentimentality, to get or screw or torment some money out of me.

I knew as we stood glaring and panting that to get the few pence he wanted he would have killed me with as little compunction as one would kill a moth which had fluttered into the room; and I knew that with as little pity I could have slaughtered him as he stood there.

He wanted sixpence, and I swore that I would see him dead before I gave it to him. He wanted twopence and I swore I would see him damned before I gave him a penny.

I moved away, but he followed me clawing my sleeve and whining:

'Twopence: you can spare twopence: what is twopence to you? If I had twopence and a fellow asked me for it I'd give it to him: twopence. . . .'

I turned and smashed my fist into his face. His head jerked upwards, and he went staggering backwards and fell backwards into the road; as he staggered the blood jetted out of his nose.

He picked himself up and came over to me bloody, and dusty, and cautious, and deprecating with a smile that was a leer . . .

'Now will you give me twopence?' he said.

I turned then and I ran from him as if I were running for my life. As I went I could hear him padding behind me, but he was in no condition, and I left him easily behind. And every time I saw him after that I ran.

Etched in Moonlight

I

He waved his pipe at me angrily:

'Words,' he said. 'We are doped with words, and we go to sleep on them and snore about them. So with dream. We issue tomes about it, and we might as well issue writs for all the information we give.'

I halted him there, for I respect science and love investigation.

'Scientists don't claim to give answers to the riddles of existence,' I expostulated, 'their business is to gather and classify whatever facts are available, and when a sufficient number of these have been collected there is usually found among them an extra thing which makes examination possible.'

'Hum!' said he.

'The difficulty lies in getting all the facts, but when these are given much more is given; for if a question can be fully stated the answer is conveyed in the question.'

'That's it,' said he, 'they don't know enough, but

there is a wide pretence—

'More a prophecy than a pretence. They really state that this or that thing is knowable. It is only that you live hurriedly, and you think everything else should be geared up to your number.

'And they are so geared, or they would not be visible and audible and tangible to me. But a ghost is geared differently to me; and I think that when I am asleep and dreaming I am geared differently to the person who is talking to you here.'

'Possibly.'

'Certainly. Look at the time it has taken you and I to chatter our mutual nonsense. In an instant of that time I could have had a dream; and, in its infinitesimal duration, all the adventures and excitements of twenty or forty years could take place in ample and leisurely sequence. Someone has measured dream, and has recorded that elaborate and complicated dreams covering years of time can take place while you would be saying knife.'

'It was du Prell,' I said.

'Whoever it was, I've seen a person awake and talking, but sleepy; noted that person halt for the beat of a word in his sentence, and continue with the statement that he has had a horrible dream. It must have taken place in the blink of an eye. There is no doubt that while we are asleep a power is waking in us which is more amazing than any function we know of in waking life. It is lightning activity, lightning order, lightning intelligence; and that is not to be considered as rhetoric, but as sober statement. The proposition being, that in sleep the mind does actually move at the speed of lightning.'

He went on more soberly:

'Last night I had a dream, and in it twenty good years were lived through with all their days and nights in the proper places; and a whole chain of sequential incidents working from the most definite beginning to the most adequate end—and perhaps it all took place between the beginning and the ending of a yawn.'

'Well, let us have the dream,' said I; 'for it is clear that you are spoiling to tell it.'

He devoted himself anew for a few moments to his pipe and to his thoughts, and, having arranged that both of these were in working order, he recommenced:

'After all this you will naturally expect that something dramatic or astonishing should follow; but it is not surprise, not even interest that is the centre of my thought about this dream. The chief person in the dream was myself; that is certain. The feeling of identity was complete during the dream; but my self in the dream was as unlike my self sitting here as you and I are unlike each other. I had a different physique in the dream; for, while I am now rather dumpish and fair and moonfaced, I was, last night, long and lean as a rake, with a black thatch sprouting over a hatchet head. I was different mentally; my character was not the one I now recognise myself by; and I was capable of being intrigued by events and speculations in which the person sitting before you would not take the slightest interest.'

He paused for a few seconds as though reviewing his memories; but, on a movement from me, he continued again, with many pauses, and with much snorings on his pipe, as though he were drawing both encouragement and dubiety from it.

'Of course I am romantically minded. We all are; the cat and the dog are. All life, and all that is in it, is romantic, for we and they and it are growing into a future that is all mystery out of a past not less mysterious; and the fear or hope that reaches to us from these extremes are facets of the romance which is life or consciousness, or whatever else we please to name it.

'But,' he said, energetically, 'I do not pine to rescue a distressed dragon from a savage maiden; nor do I dream of myself dispensing life and death and immortality with a spoon. Life is Romance; I am living and I am Romance; and that adventure is as much as I have the ability to embark on.

'Well, last night, in a dream, I was a person natively capable of such embarkations; and although I did not rescue anything from anybody, I am sure I should have done it as one to the manner born. And that character fitted me there, then, as a cat fits into its skin.

'In the dream I was unmistakably I, but I was not this I, either physically, mentally, or temperamentally.

'And the time was different. I don't know what date it was, but it was not to-day. I don't know what place it was, but it was not this place. I was acting in a convention foreign to the one we act in, and I was acting from an historical or ancestral convention which has no parallel in these times. I don't remember what language I was speaking. I don't remember the names of the people I was in contact with; nor do I recollect addressing anybody by name. I was too familiar with them to require such explanatory symbols. You and I have been chattering these years—do we ever call one another by a name? There is no need to do so; and there was no need to do so with the people of my dream.'

He halted regarding me.

'Do you believe in reincarnation?' he said.

'Do not push casual mountains on my head,' I replied, 'but get on with the dream.'

'Well,' said he, 'I dreamed a dream and here is the dream.'

II

My mind was full of disquietude, impatience, anger; and as the horse stretched and eased under me I dwelt on my own thought. I did not pursue it, for I was not actively thoughtful. I hatched it. I sat on a thought and kept it warm and alive without feeling any desire to make it grow.

'She shall end it to-day,' I thought in summary.

And then:

I'll end it to-day.

And thereon I ceased thinking, for when the will has been invoked a true, the truest, act of being has been accomplished, and the mind, which never questions the will, may go on holiday. As against willing all thought is a form of laziness, and my thought, having in that realm neither business nor interest, went lazily to the nearest simple occurrence that could employ it, and I became only a person on a horse; listening to the horse; looking at it; feeling it with my limbs and feeling myself by its aid.

There was great pleasure in the way my legs

gripped around that warm barrel: in the way my hands held the beast's head up; in the way my waist and loins swayed and curved with the swaying and curving of the animal. I touched her with my toe and tapped her neck; and on the moment she tossed her head, shaking a cascade of mane about my hands; gathered her body into a bunch of muscles, and unloosed them again in a great gallop; while from behind the hooves of my servant's beast began to smack and pelt.

In some reaches the surrounding country flowed into and over the track; and everywhere in its length the grass threw a sprinkle of green. There were holes here and there; but more generally there were hollows which had been holes, and which had in time accumulated driftage of one kind or another, so that they had a fullish appearance without having anything of a level look; but on the whole I knew of worse roads, and this one was kept in tolerable repair.

Not far from this place we left the road and struck along a sunken path all grown over at the top with shadowing trees; and so to another and much better-kept road, and on this one I shook out the reins and we went galloping.

It was not unknown to me this place. Indeed it was so well known that I had no need to look to one side or the other, for everything that was to be seen had been seen by me many hundreds of times; and, if we except grass and trees and grazing cattle, there was nothing to be seen.

Here and there rude dwellings came to view. Low shanties patched together with mud and rock, and all browned and baked by the sun and the rain; and as I rode, these small habitations became more numerous, and from them dogs and children swarmed, snarling and yelping and squeaking.

Again these fell behind, and on another turn a great park came to the view, and across it a building showed gaunt and massive, with turrets at the corners and in front, and the black silhouettes of men were moving in those airy tops.

III

My horse pulled up, all spread-eagled and snorting, before a flight of stone steps, before which and on which armed men were clustered and pacing, and I went up those steps as one having right of entry. At the top I stood for an instant to look back on the rolling grass through which I had galloped a minute before.

The evening was approaching. Ragged clouds, yet shot with sunlight, were piling in the sky, and there was a surmised but scarcely perceptible greyness in the air. Over the grass silence was coming, almost physically, so that the armed rattle and tramp and the chatter of voices about me had a detached sound, as though these were but momentary interruptions of the great silence that was on its way. That quietude, premonition of silence, brings with it a chill to the heart; as though an unseen presence whispered something, unintelligible but understood; conveying a warning that the night comes, that silence comes, that an end comes to all movements of mind and limb.

For when I parted from my horse I parted from my mood; and was again a discontented person, filled with an impatience that seethed within me as water bubbles in a boiling pot.

'She,' I thought, 'shall choose to-day whether she likes to or not.'

And, having expressed itself, my will set in that determination as a rock is set in a stream.

A person came to my beckoning finger, and replied to my enquiry—

'Your honour is expected. Will your honour be pleased to follow me?'

She was sitting in the midst of a company and on my approach gave me her hand to kiss. I saluted it half kneeling, and raking her eyes with a savage stare, which she returned with the quiet constancy to which I was accustomed and which always set me wild, so that the wish I had to beat her was only laid by the other—and overflowing—desire I had to kiss her.

I rose to my feet, stepped some paces back, and the conversation I had interrupted recommenced.

I was intensely aware of her and of myself; but saving for us the place was empty for me. I could feel my chin sinking to my breast; feel my eyes strained upwards in my bent face; feel my body projecting itself against the lips I stared at; and I knew that she was not unaware of me.

As she spoke, her eyes strayed continually to me, carelessly, irresistibly, and swung over or under me and would not look at me. She could do that while she was talking, but while she was listening she could only half do it; for when her tongue was stilled I caught her mind or her body and held her and drew her; so that, would she or would she not, she had to look at me. And I delighted in that savage impression of myself upon her; following her nerves with the cunning of one who could see within her; and guiding her, holding her, all the time to me, to me, to me. . . . And then she looked, and I was baffled anew; for her eye was as light, as calm, as inexpressive as the bright twinkle of a raindrop that hangs and shivers on a twig.

But the game was broken by a tap on my shoulder, and, at the moment, her voice stumbled on the word she was uttering, her eyes leaped into mine and looked there, and then she was talking again and merry and gracious.

It is a little difficult to explain these things for I can give no name to the people I am speaking of; nor can I say how I was known to them; but I knew their names and qualities well and they knew mine: so, at the tap on my shoulder, I, knowing whom I should see, turned my eyes to that direction, and saw, for our brows were level, a great golden head, great blue eyes and, just under the rim of vision, a great pair of shoulders.

Everything about him was great in bulk and in quality, and with the exception of our mistress, I had never met one so founded in strength and security as he was.

We turned amicably and went from the room together; out of the great building and across the fields; and as our feet moved rhythmically in the grass we smiled at each other, for indeed I loved him as my own soul and he loved me no less.

As we paced in long slow strides the darkness had already begun to be visible, for the second half of twilight was about us. Away in the direction towards which we trod an ashen sky kept a few dull embers, where, beyond sight, down on the rim of the horizon, the sun had set.

There was silence except for the innumerable rustling bred of grass and quiet trees and a wind too delicate to be heard and scarcely to be felt; for, though the skies were brisk, there was but little ground wind. Naught moved in the trees but the high tender branches that swayed lazily and all alone; leading their aery existence so far from my turbulence of passion that I chid them for their carelessness of one, who, in the very cleft of anxiety, could find an instant to remember them in.

At a time, even while we strode forward, we turned again and retraced our steps; and my mind took one shade more of moodiness. It was he had turned and not I. It was he always who did the thing that I was about to do one moment before I could do it; and he did it unthinkingly, assuredly; with no idea that rebellion might be about him; or that, being there, it could become manifest.

We re-entered and sat to meat with a great company, and she spoke to us equally and frankly and spoke to others with the gracious ease which was never for a moment apart from her.

But I, brooding on her, intent on her as with internal ears and eyes and fingers, felt in her an unwonted excitement, touched something in her which was not usual. When she looked at me that feeling was intensified; for her bright, brief glance, masked as it was and careless as it seemed, held converse with me, as though in some realm of the spirit we were in unguarded communion.

We were close together then; nearer to each other than we should be again; so close that I could feel with a pang by what a distance we might be separated; and could feel with doubled woe that she grieved for that which she could not comfort.

We left the table.

Little by little the company separated into small companies, and in a while the great room was boisterous with conversation. They had withdrawn and were talking earnestly together; and I was roving about the room, sitting for a breath with this company and that; listening to my neighbours with an ear that was hearkening elsewhere; and replying to them in terms that might or might not have been relevant to the subject I chanced on.

But in all my movements I managed to be in a position from which I could watch those two; so close in converse, so grave in their conduct of it; so alive to all that was happening about them; and yet sunk spheres below the noise and gaiety of our companions.

Her eye looked into mine, calling to me; and at the signal I left my sentence at its middle and went towards them.

Crossing the room I had a curious perception of their eyes as they watched me advancing; and, for the first time, I observed the gulf which goes about all people and which isolates each irreparably from his fellows. A sense of unreality came upon me, and, I looked on them, I looked on mystery; and they, staring at me, saw the unknown walking to them on legs. At a stroke we had become strangers, and all the apprehension of strangers looked through our eyes.

She arose when I came within a few paces of them.

'Let us go out,' said she.

And we went out quietly.

IV

Again I was in the open. I breathed deeply of the chill air as though drawing on a fount of life; as though striving to draw strength and sustenance and will into my mind.

But the time had come to put an end to what I thought of evasively as 'all this'; for I was loath to submit plainly to myself what 'all this' noted. I took my will in my hand, as it were, and became the will to do, I scarcely knew what; for to one unused to the discipline and use of will there is but one approach to it, and it is through anger. The first experience of willing is brutal; and it is as though a weapon of offence, a spear or club, were in one's hand; and as I walked I began to tingle and stir with useless rage.

For they were quiet, and against my latent impetuosity they opposed that massive barrier from which I lapsed back helplessly.

Excitement I understood and loved; the quicker it mounted, the higher it surged, the higher went I. Always above it, master of it. Almost I was excitement incarnate; ready for anything that might befall, if only it were heady and masterless. But the quietude of those left me like one in a void, where no wing could find a grip and where I scarce knew how to breathe.

It was now early night.

The day was finished and all that remembered the sun had gone. The wind which had stirred faintly in tall branches had lapsed to rest. No breath moved in the world, and the clouds that had hurried before were quiet now, or were journeying in other regions of the air. Clouds there were in plenty; huge, pilings of light and shade; for a great moon, burnished and thin, and so translucent that a narrowing of the eyes might almost let one peer through it, was standing far to the left; and in the spaces between the clouds there was a sharp scarce glitter of stars.

There was more than light enough to walk by; for that great disc of the heavens poured a radiance about us that was almost as bright as day.

Now as I walked the rage that had begun to stir within ceased again, and there crept into me so dull a lassitude that had death stalked to us in the field I should not have stepped from his way.

I surrendered everything on the moment; and, for the mind must justify conduct, I justified myself in the thought that nothing was worth this trouble; and that nothing was so desirable but it could be matched elsewhere, or done without.

It is true that the mind thinks only what desire dictates; and that when desire flags thought will become ignoble. My will had flagged, for I had held it too many hours as in a vice; and I was fatigued with that most terrible of exercises.

The silence of those indomitable people weighed upon me; and the silence of the night, and the chill of that large, white moon burdened me also. Therefore, when they came to talk to me, I listened peacefully; if one may term that state of surrender peace. I listened in a cowardly quietness; replying more by a movement of the hands than by words; and when words were indispensable making brief use of them.

It was she who spoke, and her tone was gentle and anxious and official:

'We have arranged to marry,' said she.

To that I made no reply.

I took the information on the surface of my mind as one receives an arrow on a shield, and I did not permit it to enter further. There, in neutral ground, the sentence lay; and there I could look on it with the aloof curiousity of one who examines an alien thing.

'They were going to get married!' Well . . . But what had it to do with me? Everyone got married sometime, and they were going to get married. This was a matter in which I had no part, for they were not going to get married to me: they were going to marry each other; it was all no business of mine.

So a weary brain thinks weary thoughts; and so I thought; separating myself languidly from the business of those who were making me a partner in their affairs. All I desired was that the explanations should cease, and that I might heave myself into a saddle and jog quietly to my own place.

But I knew, almost with sickness, that I could not go until this sentence had been explained and re-explained. They would inevitably consider that I could not grasp its swollen import until they had spoken under it and over it; and explained that there was a necessity for it; and detailed me that also.

I could foresee a dreary hour that would drone and drone with an unending amplification of duty and interest and love, and a whole metaphysic to bind these together.

Love! They would come to that at last. But when they dared the word they would not leave it while they had a tooth to put into it.

They would tell me around it and about; and the telling would excite them to a fury of retelling. I should have its history, and all the din and crackle of all the words that could be remembered on that subject or germain to it.

I found it happen so.

I was initiated into the secrets of their duty to their people and to themselves. I learned the intricacy of the interests wherein all parties were involved; until it was impossible to tell where duty ended and interest began. And, in the inevitable sequel, I was the confidant of their love. And I listened to that endless tale with the drowsy acquiescence of one moonstruck and gaping ... drowsily nodding; murmuring my yes and yes drowsily. . . .

They were good to me. They were sisterly and brotherly to me. By no hairsbreadth of reticence was I excluded from their thoughts, their expectations, their present felicity, and their hopes of joy to come. For two people going alone may have verbal and bodily restraint but the company of a third will set them rabid. It is as though that unnecessary presence were a challenge, or a query, which they must dispose of or die. Therefore, and because of me, they had to take each other's hand. They had to fondle paw within paw; and gaze searchingly on each other and on me; with, for me, a beam of trust and brotherliness and inclusion which my mood found sottish.

They were in love.

They whispered it to each other. They said it loudly to me. And more loudly yet they urged it, as though they would proclaim it to the moon ... And about their hands was a vile activity; a lust of catching; a fever of relinquishing; for they could neither hold nor withhold their hands from each other.

'Do they expect me to clasp their hands together, and hold them so that they shall not unloose again? Do they wish me to draw their heads together, so that they may kiss by compulsion? Am I to be the page of love and pull these arms about each other?'

We walked on, heedless of time; and I heedless of all but those voices that came to me with an unending, unheard, explanation; the voices of those who cared naught for me; who cared only that I was there, an edge to their voluptuousness.

V

But when one walks one arrives somewhere. If the environment had not changed we might have gone on for ever. This walk and talk had grown into us like a monstrous habit from which we could not break away; and until a change came to the eye our minds could not swerve from the world they were building nor our feet from the grasses we walked on.

A change did occur, mercifully; the little variety which might return that level of moonbred, love-sick continuity or inertia; for we think largely through the eyes, or our thoughts flow easily to the direction in which our gaze is set.

The great park, waving with separated trees, came

abruptly to an end.

At this step it was yet a sward. But ten paces beyond it was a rubble of bush and rock, unkempt as a beggarman's beard. Everywhere there were bits of walls with crumbling ledges up which the earth was gradually mounting and which the grass had already conquered.

Under the beam of that great flat moon the place seemed wildly beautiful; with every mound a glory of silver and peace, and every hollow a pit of blackness and mystery. A little beyond, perfect, although in the hub and centre of ruin, a vast edifice reared against the sky, and it shone white as snow in the moonlight except where a projecting battlement threw an ebon shade.

'The old castle,' said she, 'I have not walked this way in ten years.'

And, saying so, she walked to it.

I had never been that way, and I looked on that massive pile of silence almost with expectation, as though a door might open and something emerge, or a voice roar rustily at us from the moon-clad top.

It was old, and it was built as they built of old and build no more; for the walls were fifteen feet thick, and time might have sat before it through half-eternity marvelling by what arts such a solidity could possibly be reduced.

We paced about it, wondering at it, and at the silence which came to and from it; and marvelling that men had with such patience consummated so vast a labour; for the lives of generations had passed e'er this was ended and secure.

There was but one door, and we came on this in our silent walk. It was swung to, but was yet open just a little; barely a foot of opening; a dense black slit in the moonlight.

'I must slip in,' said she.

He smiled at her, catching again her hand. And into his ear, but with her eyes fixed on mine, she said:

'I want to whisper something in the ear of silence and desolation.'

She slipped within; and, when in, she pulled at his hand. With a look at me half laughing, half apologetic, he squeezed after her; and I was alone staring at the bossed and plated door.

There was silence without and within, but I found that my eyes were fixed on that silence within; and from it, as I expected, almost as I willed, there came, as though bred from the silence, a sound. It was ten times more discreet than a whisper, and was to be heard only by an ear that knew it would come.

A sudden panic leaped within my heart and rolled into my ears like a beaten drum; and that rage of fear was my memory, sprung suddenly from no-where, of the hands that had gripped and released each other; of the eyes that had flashed upon eye and lip; of the bodies that had swung tenderly sideways and fell languidly away again.

And, at that my mind emptied itself of thought, and I saw nothing, heard nothing, was nothing. Only in my head there came again a sudden great throb as though a muffled bell had thudded inside it. My hands went out without any direction from me; they gripped on the door; and, with the strength of ten men, I pulled on it.

It fell to with a crash which might have been

heard about the earth; and yet which let through one infinitesimal fraction of sound; a beginning of sound only; so tiny, it could scarcely be heard, so tense that the uproar of doom could not have covered that sound from my ear.

It began and it never finished, for it never continued. Its beginning was caught and prevented; but within my ear it continued and completed itself, as a scream which I should never cease to hear; while still with hanging jaw and fixed eyes I stared at the closed door.

I walked away.

I turned from the place and went slowly in the direction we had come.

I was a walking statue; a bodily movement only; for the man within had temporarily ceased to be. Within I was a silence brooding on silence and darkness. No smallest thought, no stir towards thinking crept in my mind; but yet I was not quite as a dead man walking, for something was happening ... I was listening. I was listening for them to speak in my heart. . . .

And then I began to run; a steady pelt of running, as though I could run away from them, mewed in that stony den, and yet liable to shriek on me from the centre of my being.

Again the change to the eye brought change to the mind; and when I sighted the great building all glimmering with lights I came to my breathless self.

I went to the stables; found my man; and in five minutes was in the saddle, and, with him behind, went plunging through the darkness towards my own place.

How often during that ride did I clench my hand

to pull on the rein and go back to release them. Every minute, every second, I was going to do it. But every minute, every second, my hand refrained from pulling on the horse, and my heels gave her notice to go yet faster.

For I was not quite a man. I was an inertia . . . or I was the horse. I was something that ran; and my whole being was an unexpressed wish to run and never stop. I did not even wish to come to my place; for, arriving there, I must halt and dismount, and fumble and totter among obstacles of doors and people. . . .

That halt had to come; and I dismounted in a mood that merged rapidly from impatience to anger, and from that to almost blind fury. In a little while my dispositions were made, and I was on the road again on a fresh beast, a bag of money and valuables strapped on the nag, and behind me two servants coming on at a gallop.

I was running away from the country. I was running away from those two mewed in the prison to which nobody knew they had gone. But more urgently even than that I was running away from myself.

VI

There comes an interval which my recollection would figure as ten or twelve years. During this time I did not return to my own country, and, so far as was possible, I did not even think of it.

For it was in my nature to forget easily; or, by an effort of the will, to prevent myself remembering whatever I considered inconvenient or distressing.

could put trouble to one side as with a gesture, and this trouble I put away and did not again admit into mind.

But a trouble that is buried is not disposed of. Be the will ever so willing, the mind ever so obedient, a memory cannot be destroyed until it has reached its due time and evolved in its proper phases.

A memory may die in the mind as peacefully as an old man dies in his bed; and it will rest there tranquilly, and moulder into true forgetfulness, as the other debris moulders into dust. But a memory cannot be buried alive; for in this state of arrested being, where it can neither grow old nor die, it takes on a perpetual unused youth, and lies at the base of one's nature as an unheard protest; calling to the nerves instead of to the brain, and strumming on these with an obstinate patience and an unending fertility of resource.

It has been banished from the surface to the depths; and in the deep of being, just beyond the borders of thought, it lies, ready as at the lifting of a finger to leap across these borders, as new and more poignant than at its creation.

Upon those having the gift of mental dismissal a revenge is taken. They grow inevitably irritable; and are subject to gusts of rage so unrelated to a present event that their contemporaries must look upon them as irresponsible.

A buried thought like a buried body will rot; and it will spread a pestilence through the moral being that is its grave or its goaler.

It was so with me.

From being one frank and impetuous and careless, I became moody, choleric, suspicious; and so temperamentally unstable that as I could not depend on myself so no one else could depend on me either.

All things that were commenced by me had to be finished by another; for in the very gust and flooding of success I would throw myself aside from it; or bear myself so outrageously that my companions would prefer failure and my absence to a success which had me within a league of the prize.

Everything, even a memory, must be faced at last. No man can rest until he has conquered or surrendered to his enemy; for, be success attained or failure, a legitimate bourne is reached wherein the mind may acquiesce and be at one with the result.

So, one day, I unburied my dead; looking upon it with a curiosity and fear which were the equal of each other; and having once looked I could not forbear to look again; until I became a patient, timid devotee of my own evil.

A treacherous story in truth; and if repentance could have retrieved my crime how quickly it had been erased. But the fact of repentance comes home only to the person in fault. It has no value for the victim; for a man may outrun the laws of man, but the law of his self he can neither distance nor dodge.

Half the value of an act is its reaction, for the one pays and completes the other. My act was vanity and here came shame to make of it a total; and there, in the mixture of the two, was I, fully expressed and condemned. Vanity had sentenced me to shame; and shame would take up the tale again with vanity, and would lead me to the further justice of which I had need. For that which we do outwardly we do inwardly. We condemn or reward ourselves in every action; and the punishment we receive is due to us in a sense deeper than that indicated in the word retribution.

I thought of those two; and I thought of them shyly as one who no longer had the right even to remember them. For they had counted on my nature, as they judged it; on my honour as they knew it; and on my friendship as they thought to have proved it. But into these aspects of me they had been sucked as into a bog. I had given way under their feet and they had sunk into and died in me.

Was it a wonder that I fled across the fields fearful lest they might scream to me from my soul? Alas, it was there they had been betrayed, and there were buried; wherever else their bones might whiten.

And now I began to brood on them deeply and perpetually, until nothing in the world was so important as they were, and they became me almost in my entirety.

I reconstructed them and myself, and the happy days which had preceded that most wicked of hours; and I knew that, whatever other enmity or suspicion had been in the world, there had been nought but friendship between us and the frankest and freest trust. I had reason to trust them, and had given them occasion to believe that in my keeping their honour and their all was safe; and to that trust I had given the lie at the moment of its reposal.

Indeed I was stupefied to think that I had committed this baseness; for on behalf of these two I would have counted on my own loyalty with as little calculation as they had.

There was indeed something to be said for me if that enquiry were rigorously pursued. But it was a poor thing and only to be advanced in my favour for it could not be urged.

She had halted between us for a long time; not balancing our values or possibilities; but humanly unwilling to judge, and womanly unable to wound. That delicate adjustment could not have continued indefinitely; but it would have continued longer had I not forced the issue, or stated the position; and once that a case is truly stated nothing remains but the judgement which is already apparent in the statement.

It was I had failed in the trial. I whose nerves gave way. I who became impatient and would gamble on the chance; and the gambler is always an incomplete man. In all real things the gambler must lose, for he is staking on chance that which can only be won by the knowledge which is concreted merit; and in all memorable deeds the personality must win, and chance have not even the ghost of a chance.

They had bettered me; and, although they were dead and I alive, they were beyond me and topped me as a lion tops a dog.

So, pride having proved to me that I was treacherous, shame came to teach me the great lesson of life; for in humility the mind is released from fleshy fogs and vapours; and in that state only can it be directed to its single natural work, the elucidation of character.

Ideas which enter the mind only have no motive force—they are alive, but have not yet energy. They exist but as subjects of conversation, as intellectual gossip, but before a thought can become an act it must sink deeper than the mind and into the imagination where abides the true energy of all thinking creatures. It is not the mind but the imagination that sets the will to work; and both mind and will obey it instantly, as a horse winces instantly to the touch of a spur.

So these two, having got into my imagination, could not be let out again, until it was satisfied that all which could be done was done, and a moral as well as a logical end arrived at.

I took to horse, therefore, and set out for home.

VII

Apart from my adventure with those people my memory is blurred. My dealings and encounters with them are distinct as though they happened to-day; but the portions of the narrative interspacing that adventure have already more than half faded from memory. Yet it seems to me that my journey back was a long one, and that ships had to be taken as well as horses ere I had returned and could recognise landmarks and faces.

In many of these recognitions the passage of time was marked for me as though it had been written.

Here was a dwelling which had not before been here: and in this place, where a house had been, there was a roofless ruin.

Here a man tended his sheep. When I passed the last time he had not been old; but his beard had whitened as though in one night of snow.

I passed youths and girls who knew me and stood aside; but they had changed from the children I might have remembered into lusty and lengthy and unknown people.

The word that I was coming must have far preceded me, for these people recognised me with curiosity but without astonishment; and in my own house I was clearly expected and welcomed with all the preparedness a master might hope for.

I had not hoped for any welcome, and would have preferred to come back as anonymously as a bird does who returns to its last year's hedge; for, although I did not wish to escape anything that might be in keeping for me, I did desire to inform myself of the circumstances by which I should be surrounded, and the dangers that I might have to front.

There was no hint of danger or disquietude among my people. Their welcome was as free, their service as easy and accustomed as though I had returned from a visit to the next town. And the marvel of this almost stupefied me; while the impossibility of demanding direct information from those unsuspicious people plunged me in dismay.

I thought to myself—'The bodies have never been found, and, by some extraordinary chance, suspicion has not turned upon me for their disappearance.'

At the thought a weight was lifted from my soul; but only for a moment; for I had not come back in search of security, but in order that whatever debt was due by me should be paid.

But I had to know how things were, and, after

eating, the man of whom I enquired, replied that my return was known at the Castle (as I shall call it) and that a visit from its chatelains was expected on the next day to welcome me home.

With this news my alarm vanished and an almost excessive joy took its place. My mind lightened, and poured into my body, as from a fountain, well-being and energy.

For how long? Was it more than ten minutes? ten seconds? The mind that can hold joy must be strong indeed. I could no more contain it than I could round the sea in my palm; and, almost as it had swirled into me, it swept out; leaving behind only that to which I had a right and which was my own.

Nothing happens without mental acquiescence, and that which had emptied my mind of joy and my body of buoyancy was the memory that I should see them on the morrow, and, with that memory, egotism pushed up its head and I thought—'they will not meet the unfledged youngster they parted from!'

That was all. But it was sufficient to ride me as I would ride a horse, and to pull me round to its direction, and to the vanity I imagined to have left behind.

I chid myself for a fool. I looked back with a lightning eye on the wasted years; the useless misery; the unnecessary toil and sordid excitement through which I had passed; and at a stroke my mind became filled with a tumult and admixture of emotions which no one word would synthesise, nor could I describe them in many words.

In undisciplined minds a conflict of thought will

provoke anger or sleep; but in almost any mind a conflict of emotion will breed rage; and, for the mind is lazy, a thought will seek for an emotion to rest on, and will lie in it as in a bed. So nobility rots in dream, and action grows stagnant in imagining itself. Behind life is laziness, and from it, in direct descent or ascent, is desire and lust and anger, which master words describe up to a point the world and its working.

Thus, having torn myself out of anger as from a pit, I hurried back to it, and I found that I was thinking of my coming visitors with a dislike which was as near to hatred as I could arrive at.

They were alive, and I had paid for their death! I had wasted myself and my years grieving for them; repenting for them; idealising them in a dull torment and agitation of nerve and brain!

For nothing! And nothing became symbolised by them. They stood for it: they were Nothing; and, with that, vanity was in possession again, for I stood for something as against their nothing; and all the coil of pride and shame and payment had to recommence.

VIII

They came, and for a time resentment was covered by curiosity; and while we talked together I found myself glancing at one and the other with the curiosity of him who peeps at a camel or a criminal.

There was a difference in them, but it was not essential; it was only the change which comes with the passage of time.

All that I remembered was here, but more pronounced. What had been quietude had deepened to tranquillity. All that sense of certainty and command was more certain and commanding, for ease and power and good humour was as unconsidered and native a part of them as their limbs.

He had been great in bulk, he was now huge. He had filled out, and filled in, and he strode and towered like a mountain.

Her I remembered as one remembers a day of April beauty and promise, various with that uncertainty which troubles and delights. Now summer was on her with all its gorgeous endowment.

She was a rest to the eye. She was a benediction to the senses. She calmed desire. For to look on her was to desire no more, and yet to be satisfied. Her beauty was so human, her humanity so beautiful, that she could embrace the thought that would embrace her; and return it absolved, purified, virgin again to the lust that sent it out.

There are beings in this world who are secured against every machination of evil. They live as by divine right, as under divine protection; and when malice looks in their faces it is abashed and must retreat without harming them. All the actions of these are harmonious and harmless and assured; and in no circumstances can they be put in the wrong, nor turned from their purpose. Their trust is boundless, and, as they cannot be harmed, so it cannot be betrayed. They are given their heaven on earth as others are here given their hell; and what they get they must have deserved; and they must indeed be close to divinity.

Of such were these, and I hated them with a powerlessness which was a rage of humility; and I mourned for myself as the hare may mourn who is caught in a trap and knows that it will kill him.

I did not hate them, for they could not be hated. My egotism envied them. My shame, and, from it, my resentment, was too recent to be laid, though the eyes of a dove looked into mine and the friendliest hand was on my shoulder. Something obstinate within my soul, something over which I had no charge, stiffened against them; and if one part of my nature yearned for surrender and peace the other part held it back, and so easily that there was never a question as to where obedience must go.

I was easy with them and as careless as I had ever been; and the fact that I had not harmed them put out of my mind the truth that I had tried to do so. Not by a look, an intonation, did they show a memory of that years'-old episode; and what they could forget I could forget as quickly; or could replace by the recollection that in a distant time they had set me adrift in a world of torment.

This did not express itself even in my mind. It lay there like a bulk of unthought thought; which, as it was expressed in its entirety and not in its parts, had to be understood by the nerves where the intelligence lacked width and grasp; and there was I again in the trough of the sea and twisting to any wind.

In a little time I had reaccustomed myself to the new order of things. The immediate past of wandering and strife grew less to be remembered, and my new way of life became sequential and expected.

I knew, and there is contentment in that kind of knowledge, exactly what I should do on the morrow; and I might have ventured a prediction as to how I should be employed in the month to come. For life gathered about me in a web of unhasty occupation and untiring leisure; so that the thing to be done and the doing of it flowed sweetly to each other; and all was accomplished without force, and almost without volition.

Many times my horse took that well-remembered road, and it became as natural to me to turn in that direction as to turn to the rooms of my own house. For I found there much that I desired, even unconsciously: friendship, companionship, and, more than all, gaiety; for their young lusty brood began to knit themselves about my life and knot themselves into it.

To go from a sedate, unruffled house into a home that seethes with energy and innocence, and all the animation of budding life, is a notable thing for one who has come to the middle term; and though he had before suffered children with a benevolent impatience he grows to be thankful if they will notice him with even an approach to interest.

It is a blessed thing that whoever wishes to be welcomed benevolently by a child will be so welcomed; for the order of young years is to respond, and they do that without reservation. Children and animals, however we can hurt, we cannot hate; for they are without reserve; and that lack is the one entirely lovable quality in the world.

In the meantime events moved with me, for they, having settled their own lives, charged themselves with the arrangement of mine; and, by a delicate, untiring management, I found myself growing more friendly or more accustomed to a lady of her kin; whom at last, they expected me to marry; who certainly expected to marry me; and whom I should wed when the time came with neither reluctance nor impatience. But this lady I do not remember even slightly. She is a shade; a fading smile, and exists for me as a dream within the dream.

It was settled, and whether I or they or she arranged it I no longer know. It may have been just propinquity, or that sense of endlessness, that inertia of speech, which causes one to continue talking when there is no more to be said; so that, and inevitably, one asks a girl to marry one, there being nothing left to be said; and she, terrified lest silence should fall upon her, agrees to do so, and marvels thereat until she is endlessly wed.

So I asked and she replied; and those who take charge of such arrangements took charge of this; and settled all about time and place, and removed every impediment to our union.

IX

It was the night before my wedding, and I was filled with that desolation of the traveller who must set forth on the morrow, and does not quite know where he is going, nor why he should go there. I had, as was now my custom, taken horse and gone to the castle. The girl I should marry was there, and those two who walked like gods on the earth and who stirred like worms in my mind.

We talked and ate, but beyond that I can only remember the atmosphere of smiles and kindliness to which I was accustomed.

My recollection begins towards nightfall. I had kissed that girl's hands and she went away to her bed; and I was preparing to perform the same duty to my hostess, when she postponed it.

'It is a lovely night,' she said, 'and,' looking at her husband meaningly, as I thought, 'after to-morrow we three shall not be the companions we have been. We shall not meet so often nor so carelessly.'

To my glance of enquiry she continued, smilingly:

'A husband belongs to his wife. Your leisure will henceforth have so many claims on it that we may see little of you. When we see you again we may, like drunken men, see you double.'

My glance was humorous but questioning.

'Let us take a last walk,' she suggested.

'Yes,' her husband assented. 'One more walk of comrades; one more comfortable talk, and then let to-morrow work what changes it may.'

It was a lovely night, with a sky swept bare of all but the moon.

High in the air, bare and bright and round, she rode in beauty.

And, but for her, we might have seen how lonely was the blue serene that swung about her.

Naught stayed in that immense for eye or ear. Naught stirred or crept. All slept but sheer, clear space and silence. And they, with the wonder of the wide, high heaven, were wonderful.

Afar, apart, in lovely alternating jet and silver, the sparse trees dreamed. They seemed as turned upon themselves. As elves they brooded; green in green; whisht and inhuman and serene.

All moved within.

All was indrawn.

All was infolded and in solitude.

The sky, the grass, the very earth rejected knowing; and we hied with the moon as though she and we were atune to naught beside.

Against that blank withdrawal we struggled as the uneasy dead may, who would regain a realm in which they can find no footing. Silence came on us as at a command; and we were separated and segregated, each from the other, and from all things, as by a gulf.

I looked to the faces on either side of me. They were thin and bright and utterly unknown to me. They seemed wild and questing; stern-poised eagle profiles that were alien in every way to the friendly faces I had known.

And I! I could not see my own face, but I could feel it as a blanch of apprehension.

Why should fear thus flood my being? For there was nothing within me but fear. I was a blank that swirled with terror; and was stilled as suddenly to a calmness scarcely less terrifying. I strove to engage my thoughts in common things, and, with that purpose, I scanned on every side so that my mind might follow my eye and be interested in its changes.

But in the moonlight there is no variety. Variety is colour, and there was about me but an universal shimmer and blanch, wherein all shape was suppressed, and nothing was but an endless monotony and reduplication of formless form.

So we went; and in the quietude we paced through and the quietness we brought with us we scarce seemed living beings.

We were spectres going in a spectral world. Although we walked we did not seem to move; for to that petrified universe our movement brough no change; and each step was but an eddy in changeless space.

I looked at them; at those faces cut by the moon to a sternness of stone; and I knew in a flash that I was not going between friends but between guards; and that their intention towards me was pitiless.

My will was free. I could have turned and walked backwards, and they would not have hindered me in any way. But they might have smiled as they turned, and that smile would be deadly as an arrow in the heart.

To dare be a coward how courageous one must be! I thought with envy of those whose resolution is so firm that they can fly from danger while there is yet a chance. But to be a coward and to be afraid to save oneself! Into what a degradation must one have fallen for that!

I clenched my hands, and at the contact of my nails I went cold to the bone.

X

At a certain moment each of those silver-pale faces seemed to look forward more straitly, more distantly; and I, withdrawing my eyes from the grey-toned vegetation at my feet, looked forward also.

We had reached the extreme of the park. Beyond was a rugged, moon-dozed tumble of earth and bush and rock; and beyond again was the vast silver-shining keep, to which, in years long gone, we three had walked; and from which, and in what agony, I once had fled.

In the miracle we call memory I recovered that

night, and was afflicted again with the recollection of clasping and unclasping hands, of swaying bodies, and of meeting and flying eyes.

But the same hands made now no mutual movement. Those eyes regarded nothing but distance; and those bodies but walked and did no more. It was my hands that twitched and let go; my eyes that stared and flinched away; my body that went forward while its intuition and intention was to go back.

In truth I did halt for a heart's beat; and when I moved again, I was a pace in advance, for they had stayed on the instant and could not move again so quickly as my mood drove.

I looked at them no more. I looked at nothing. My eyes, although wide, were blind to all outward things, and what they were seeking within me it would be hard to tell.

Was I thinking, or feeling or seeing internally? For I was not unoccupied. Somewhere, in unknown regions of my being, there were busynesses and hurryings and a whole category of happenings, as out of my control as were the moods of those who went with me.

All thought is a seeing. No idea is real if it be not visualised. To see is to know; to know is to see clearly, and other knowledge than that is mechanical. But as we cannot see beyond a stated range of vision so we cannot speak beyond a definite range of thought. Fear has never uttered itself; nor has joy; nor any emotion that has quickened beyond normality. These stir in a mood too remote for expression by words that are fashioned to tell the common experiences of sense and its action.

How should I tell that which was happening to me as I trod forward; my face as impassive as theirs, my brow as calm? The reaction to extreme events is in the spine or the pit of the stomach, but the action is elsewhere, and is in an organ uncharted yet by man.

I trod with them, free to all appearance as a man can be, and yet bound by fetters which had been forged through long years by myself for myself.

We halted, and I looked again on the bossed and monumental door which stood in my memory almost as a living thing. It was as it had been formerly. A black gape, little more than a foot wide, yawned from the top to the bottom. I noticed the rough herbage sprouting grossly among pebbles at its foot, and the overhanging jut of harsh stone that crowned or frowned from its top. And then I looked at them.

His gaze was bent on me, massive as the stone itself.

'Go in,' he said.

I looked at her, and although her lips said nothing her eyes, gleaming whitely in the moonlight, commanded as sternly as her husband's voice.

'Go in,' he said harshly, 'as we went in, and get out, if you can, as we got out,'

He reached a monstrous hand to my shoulder; but, at my motion to put it aside, he let it fall; and instead his hand took hold of the great knob. I cast one look at the vast, white moon; at the steady blue spaces about it; at the tumbled sparkle that was the world; and, without a word, I squeezed through the narrow aperture.

I turned and looked back. I had one glimpse of a

black form set in a dull radiance. Then the door closed on me with a clang that echoed and echoed and echoed in my ears long after its cause had ceased.

XI

It was dark where I was.

It was a darkness such as I had never experienced. The blackness about me was solid as ebony. It was impenetrable to thought itself.

It flooded my brain so that the blindness within me was as desperate as that without. I could not keep my eyes open; for, being open, they saw the darkness. I dared not close them; for, being closed, I became that darkness myself. . . .

And at every moment, from the right hand and the left, from before me and from behind me, I imagined things. Darknesses that could move, silences that could touch. . . .

I dared not realise my speculations, and yet, in lightning hints, my mind leaped at and fled from thoughts that were inexpressible except as shivers. My flesh twitched and crept, and I shrank from nothing, as though it could extend a claw; as though it could clutch me with an iron fist. . . .

I was standing yet, long after they had gone, beside the door; fearing to move from it; afraid to stir; and looking about me, as it were, with my ears.

I had no anger against them. I was too occupied for any emotion but those, or that, which was present. I ceased even to think about them; or such seconds of thought as chanced through my agony were humble. They were not forgiving or regretful;

they were merely humble, as the thoughts of an overdriven sheep might be towards its driver.

They were gone; and with them everything had gone. I was surrounded by nothingness. I was drowned in it. I was lost and solitary as some grey rock far out in sea. Nay, for the sun shines on it, the wind blows, and a gannet halts there and flaps his wing. There was loneliness nowhere but where I was. There was not such a silence even in the tomb as the silence in which I was centred; for, while the terror of darkness did not diminish, the horror of silence began to grow. And it grew as some monstrous thing may that reproduces itself on itself, tirelessly, timelessly, endlessly.

Nature abhors a vacuum, and so does the mind, for the mind is nature. It will contrive sound when silence oppresses it, and will people any desolation with its own creatures. Alas for man! With what pain he can create how meagre a joy! With what readiness he can make real a misery!

And my ears had two duties to perform! They must look for me as well as listen, and when the mind is occupied in two endeavours something of craziness comes, even in trivial things.

I began to hear, and at no time could I tell what I heard. I began to see, and no words will impart what I saw. I closed both eyes and ears with my fingers, and was aware in a while that my under-jaw was hanging; that my mouth was open; and that I was listening and looking through that.

At the knowledge my will awakened, and I placed calmness forcibly on myself as though I were casing my soul in mail. I strode firmly to my right hand, and after a few steps I came against a wall. I strode in the opposite direction, and in double the paces I came against a wall. I walked backwards, and in twenty steps I came against a wall; and following this my groping fingers tapped suddenly in space.

There was an aperture. . . .

My hair rose on my head stiff and prickling. I did not dare to enter that void in the void. I should more willingly have leaped into a furnace. I went from it on tip-toe, striving to make no sound lest that hole should hear me, and tread behind. . . .

It would come noiselessly. And yet it would be heard! It would roll gently, overwhelmingly, like some new and unimaginable thunder.

'No . . . !' I said in panic to my soul, as I trod cautiously from that behind.

'Great God!' I thought, as I stood somewhere, for now I had lost all direction, and was nowhere. 'Great God, what shall I do?'

I lowered myself secretly to the ground, groping with a blind hand to make sure that nothing was there.

'I will try to sleep,' I said in my mind.

Nay, I said it to my mind; striving to command that which I had never learned to control. I huddled my knees up and curved my chin forward like a sleeping dog. I covered my face with my hands, and was still as the stone on which I lay.

'I will try to sleep,' I said. 'I will think of God,' I said.

And it seemed to me that God was the blankness behind, which might advance. And that nothing was so awful as the thought of Him—unimaginable and real! withheld, and imminent, and threatening, and terrific! My knees were listening for Him to the front of me: my back was hearkening from behind; and my brain was engaged elsewhere in matters which I could not cognise.

'If I were to speak aloud!' I thought.

And some part of my mind dared me to do so; wheedled at me to utter one clapping shout: but I knew that at the sound of a voice, of even my own voice, I should die as at a stroke.

XII

How long did that last? Was it an hour, a year, a lifetime?

Time ceases when emotion begins, and its mechanical spacings are then of no more account. Where is time when we sleep? Where is it when we are angry? There is no time, there is but consciousness and its experiences.

I stayed where I had lain myself, and whether my eyes were open or closed I no longer knew. The miseries of this place had abated. No, that does not express it, for this was no longer a place. This place had disappeared, or it had been merged in the new dimension which I call Nowhere.

It is immeasurably great; it is unimaginably small: for as there is no time so there is no space: there is only being, and its modes: and in that region my misery continued itself far from the knowledge of this brain and beyond the let or hindrance of this body.

And yet somewhere, somehow, I knew something that I can only think of as nothing. An awful, a deadly business was proceeding, with me as the subject. It can only be expressed negatively. Thus I may phrase it, I had gone in the spirit into that aperture from which I had fled. I was in contact with the unmanifest, and that, in its own sphere, is as competent and enduring as are its extensions with which we are familiar. But of that I cannot speak; for as it was out of range of these senses so it was out of range of this mind whose sole pre-occupation is these senses.

I had been in terror, but in what was I now? How little to me was the human absence of light, the normal absence of sound that had frightened me.

I was nowhere, and it was real. I was nothing and I was enduring. I would have returned to my blank, dumb prison as one flies to a paradise, but I could not, for something had happened to me. I was translated; and until that experience was fulfilled I could not regain myself nor evade in any way my happenings.

Therefore, I do not know how long I remained crouched in that stony den. Nor how I lay; nor aught that happened to me. But at a point I did return to normal consciousness, and that as swiftly as though one had taken me by the shoulders and clicked me to another direction.

All that monstrous Something-Nothing ceased; and I was listening with these ears, and staring through known darkness with these eyes that see you.

There were footsteps outside the door, and in an instant the door grinced and screeched and swung.

XIII

It was those two. But I did not move from where I

lay, and when I did so it was because he lifted me. Those giant arms could lift me as one plucks up a cat; and in a moment I was walking, and the arm that was yet around my waist was pressing me lovingly to his side.

'We were only playing with you,' he said.

And she at my other side cooed, as she fondled my hand.

'It was only a game.'

I looked wordlessly from one to the other and laughed gently.

It was strange that I did not wish to speak. It was stranger still that I would not speak; and to everything that they said I returned my gentle laugh. That, it seemed to me, must be sufficient communion even for them; and who in the world could wish to speak when he might laugh?

We walked on, slowly at first, and then hastily, and sentences came from one to the other across me; sometimes explanations, at times assertions and assents.

'It took us ten minutes to get out,' he said, 'and we thought—'

'For you are so much cleverer than we are,' she interposed.

'That you would have been home almost as quickly as we were.'

'It took us ten long minutes to imagine that although the door was closed it might not be fastened,' he went on, 'but when I pulled on it it opened at once.'

'I was glad to see the moonlight,' he continued in a tone of reverie.

'Glad!' she exclaimed.

'Those ten minutes were unpleasant,' he assented.

'They were wicked,' she exclaimed energetically. 'They—' she paused and took my arm again: 'They are forgotten and forgiven. Our thoughts of each other now can be all frankness and trust.

I must have been imprisoned for some hours, for when I went in there had been a bright moon in a bare sky, where now there was no moon and the heavens were deeply shadowed. Our faces were visible to each other as dull shapes, and the spaces about us were bathed in that diaphanous darkness through which one looks without seeing, and against which things loom rather than show.

A wonderful feeling of well-being flowed through me, warming and bracing me. A feeling of astonishing rest for myself, and of endless affection for my companions.

And with it all there was a sense, confused and yet strong, that I knew something which they did not know. That I had a secret which would astonish them when they discovered it.

I knew they should discover it, for I would reveal it to them myself, as soon as I became aware of what it really was. And my mind was filled with joy at the thought of how I would surprise them, and of how they should be surprised.

That strange knowledge lay like a warmth at my heart. It lit the dull night for me, so that through the gloom and mirk I walked as on air and in radiance. All that I had gone through vanished from my memory. It was as though it had never been. Nothing was any more but this new-found rest and contentment.

Happiness! I had found it at last; and it was more worth finding than anything I had yet experienced.

But the end of our walk was nigh. At a distance was the gleam of lights, and black silhouettes about them. We increased our pace, I, willingly enough, for I wished to tell them a secret; and in a short time we came to the great steps and mounted them. Men were there with torches, and we walked gaily from darkness into light.

Reaching the top, on the wide platform before the door, she turned to me with a smile, and she stopped dead. I saw the smile frozen on her face. I saw her face blanch to the whiteness of snow, and her eyes widen and fix and stare. She clasped her bosom with both hands and stood so, staring.

Then something, a self of me, detached itself from me, and stood forward and looked also.

I saw myself. My mouth was twisted sidewards in a jolly grin. My eyes were turned inwards in a comical squint, and my chin was all a sop of my own saliva.

I looked at myself so for a mortal moment, and I awakened.

Darling

Old Four Eyes was quite young. That is, he was about thirty-three or four years of age, but there are people who are born middle-aged, and he was one of them: he was called 'old' for that reason; and he was called 'Four Eyes' because he wore spectacles.

He had attained to all the dignity which the average man can hope for, that is, he was married and he had a situation. In the latter he had reached the emolument beyond which the average man does not dare to covet; that is, he had thirty-five shillings a week.

He had married his wife very largely because there was no one else who could so easily be married; and she, after attending quite a respectable time, had married him because no one better had turned up.

It was not that any particular urgency of the blood drove them to each other's arms; for they could not have mustered one infantile passion

194

between them. It was that one married at a certain time after leaving school. It is one of the things that are done. They lived on the same tram-line. They went to the same Church. They attended the same semi-clerical or lay clerical meetings and missions which every Church fosters. They were thus continually meeting, and at last saluting, and at long last, through the introduction of a clergyman, speaking.

He saw her home once: he saw her home again: then he always saw her home.

Why did they go to Church? It was not to praise God—they would not have known how to do such a thing. It was not to pray—their characters were not strong enough for such an exercise of intellect and will. They went to Church because they had gone there when they were children; because it was the proper thing to do; because Church and its accessories formed a Society in which they could mix, and which rescued them from the feeling of individuality and detachment which can so easily become a sense of utter loneliness and despair.

When two young people have convoyed each other home in the late hours they must do the right thing, that is, they must get married: and so these two got married.

Love! There was none of it. Even affection does not seem to be necessary for such a coupling. Of course, they had both read the right books, and from these had gleaned that love existed and that affection was a postulate for matrimony. To be loving was, therefore, the right thing to be, and they loved as in duty bound. They said 'darling' to each other frequently, and, although less frequently, they clasped each other's hands.

They had a wedding party—they both saved up for it from their very meagre wages—and to the wedding a dozen people of their own tribe were invited, and were regaled on lemonade and buns: there were other and more notable meats than these. The proper speeches were made; the proper toasts were drained in bubbling and hissing glasses. Everything, they told each other afterwards, went off splendidly, and they went away to a seaside place for six days.

They they returned to the small house they had taken and furnished on the instalment system, and thus they became man and wife, and the one flesh.

II

For a week or two they were almost excited. Their meals were no longer solitary. Each night they shared a supper and a bed. They walked arm in arm to Church twice every Sunday, and thus enlinked they walked back together and did not separate on arriving at a door.

When the morning tea was prepared, she would call out:

'Breakfast is ready, darling.'

And when he was going to work he would say:

'Did you notice where I left my hat, darling?'

She did not go to work any more, for that was not the thing; and when he came home in the evening he listened dutifully to the conversation which she had accumulated during a companionless day.

Indeed, he sometimes thought she talked for longer than was necessary about the way the kitchen tap dripped. When it was turned off it did not entirely turn off.

At first he admired and envied her ease in speech; for he could not at all have uttered so many words about a water tap. He marvelled at her. Each night brought its own subject. It might be about the fading oilcloth on the hall: it might be about cockroaches in the basement: it might be that the silk in her wedding-present umbrella had slit. On these subjects, on all and every subject, she was able to emit unceasing and perfectly grammatical phrases.

He sat with her in the parlour and hearkened diligently to her tale. He would lie silent in bed, and, long after the candle had been blown out, he would stretch beside her in the darkness, and would listen, listen, listen.

He could not help listening, and the thin sound of his wife's voice began to beat on his ear as something monstrously dull, as an eternal, inexplicable, complaint.

He almost regretted having got married.

III

He had a long-haired thin-grown moustache. He had a large badly cut nose. He had dull blue eyes which stared, as though he were listening with them instead of with his ears. He had as little chin as could be without having no chin at all. His ears swung slightly outwards. The ends of his trousers flopped about his ankles, and from the flop and waggle of these garments one knew that his legs were as skinny as matches. One divined that his elbows were sharp enough to wear a hole through his coat, and that his feet were longish and flattish and that his toes mounted energetically on top of each other.

One knew that he was less protected against life than a snail is. One knew that one could do anything one pleased to him without fear; and that, unless the thing done was terribly public, he would not even complain.

His wife knew it, but she had only blood enough for the little, bitter dislike which flowed from her in a thin, bitter, unceasing sound of words.

He liked everyone in the world. He liked everything in the world. He liked anything. That, if he had an ambition, was all his ambition, to be let like people; to be let placate people, and to let them see that he liked them.

Never was such a handshake as he gave. It seemed he would never again let go of one's fingers. Never did eyes beam on one with such entire assurance that here was goodwill. That here was one who would be gratified by your good fortune. That here was one who would laugh and perform antics like a dog if that would give you pleasure. That here was one who implored you not to do him harm.

IV

Life flowed on.

Three years of the slab of nonsense which he called life went by; and he was alive, a little bonier than before, but with an imperceptible growth of boniness that left him unchanged to himself.

He was more eager than ever when he clasped your hand in both of his own, and clung to it as thinking that here might be safety. On your approach he wagged his tail with a woeful energy; and his dumb eyes implored you to take him away with you, and feed him. To tie him up, if you had the heart to do that, but to take him away with you, and not let him stray any longer.

For he was terribly afraid. He had lost all hope, and he saw the end coming to him irresistible as death. He saw the calamity and disaster to which he was fated coming on him implacably, and he wanted to be let off: he wanted a corner where he could lay his bones on straw and blink at the sun.

For he was tired; and could no longer work as he used to work. His wife's voice, that unceasing, bitter little drone, came between him and his work: it drowned all his thoughts: it destroyed the mere mechanical remembrance which was his work. He could no longer be certain that his tots at the end of the ledger were right. He could not remember the thing which he had been told to remember for to-morrow; for she droned into his ear in the middle of the column of figures; and she buzzed at him while his superior was giving him instructions.

The other men began to play pranks on him.

They filled his ink bottle with lumps of blotting paper, so that when he lifted out the pen he would put a two-inch blot on the ledger. They stole his cup at the lunch hour and he found in its place a cup full of red ink. They turned his desk upside down: tore his papers, bashed in his hat; spread gum on his chair. They did everything to him which careless, malevolent minds could think of, knowing that as he did not know whom to complain of he would never complain.

Things began to get unbearable. Not unbearable for him; for until death came he could bear anything. Things began to get unbearable for his masters. They did not know who played the pranks, but they knew all about the pranks; and as his incompetence became more evident so their speech to him became more short, their looks more dissatisfied.

In the face of these things he could return and return, but he could not battle; he could oppose there nothing but his eagerness to please and his dumb eyes.

He saw his dismissal coming; and with it he saw the end of life, the fading away of the green earth, and the going out of the sun. He strove against his dismissal with humility, and further than his abjectness humility itself could not go.

It was a thing of shame; and God knows he was ashamed. It was obscene; and perhaps God counted his tears as they slid burning and tickling along that gaunt nose into his moustache.

V

He was dismissed, and he stood before his master as a sheep might stand before its butcher. He listened without a word and went away without a word.

His wife droned and droned and droned. But now it was not only in the night time; the dark cavern of thin, unintermitting sound. She had all the day to talk in and all the night; and both the day and the night were filled by her with words.

He fled from the house. He walked up streets and down streets; pushing open shop doors, office doors, and doors of stables and yards, seeking employment; carrying his frightened eyes and his humility into every sort of place and every kind of company.

But he might as fruitfully have asked for employment from the winds and the waters. There was no employment for him on the earth. There was no place for him under the wide canopy of heaven.

The little money he had managed to save vanished away.

The people from whom he had hired his furniture came with a van and took it away again. His wife went away to live with a cousin until she could find work.

For a few days and nights he roved about the empty house; eating stale crusts that he found, drinking water from the tap, sleeping on the rubbish-littered floor. Then one morning the landlord knocked and asked for the keys. He gave them and the landlord saw him off the premises.

He was in the street, and he had nothing in the world but a pair of spectacles.

He stared through them at the clouds. He looked at the clouds fixedly as he paced forward, thinking that maybe he would see God through his spectacles.

The Wolf

I

One had but to look at his face to know that he was
a quiet man. Indeed, he was the quietest man in the
village. There were some who carried that modest
statement further and maintained that he was the
quietest man in the world; but these people, as we
say, go beyond the beyonds.

He was tallish, without being tall; he was thinnish,
without being skinny; he had pale blue eyes which
seemed as though they had been glazed after they
were put in; he had light fair hair that plastered itself down in the places where it could be seen, and
stuck a surreptitious hair or so up in the places
where they could not be seen. His feet turned inwards; not much it is true, but whatever turn might
be to them was inwards; and although his knees did
not knock together when he walked still they nearly knocked together. His ears were put on so un-
handily that you might have sworn he put them on
himself, and a glance told you that he was an un-

handy man.

When you looked at him first you thought of a sheep; but on a second glance you racked your brains to think of some animal which was not quite so larky as a sheep. Does not a sheep carry itself with a certain timid dignity? And it has a robust curiosity to boot.

He did not seem to be married, but he was, and he had the right wife. The neighbours said so, after-wards, and the saying gave her a modified popularity.

Her sole claim to note before that had been that every time she came close enough to her husband's head she hit it. She hit it with anything that was handy—a potstick, a saucepan, her fist, anything.

It was not that she disliked her husband's head. It was more that she did not see it, or that she saw something which seemed to be eternally in her way. That she hit, and shooed out of doors as she would have shooed out an enterprising, unnecessary chicken.

When a chicken is hit it squawks and rustles and runs, a brief feathery uproar; but when he was struck he just went; he faded; he was gone.

His wife didn't know he had gone; she didn't know he had come; she didn't know she had hit him.

He was a quiet, quiet man.

That being so, one was the more stupefied when he was brought before the magistrates, and folk unerringly, unanimously, remembered the name of the animal they could not recall, when they said he was not exactly like a sheep, but that he was more like one of them . . . one of them what-do-you-callthems.

'Hasn't he the look of a wolf?' said the people, 'a wolf with softening of the brain?'

And everyone was satisfied, for they had a name on him at last.

They said, 'Wait until he does his six months' hard and the wife gets a grip of him.'

II

There was a fair at Carroll's Pass five miles away.

To get to Carroll's Pass from where he lived you turned to the east and walked straight in front of you through a narrow valley; a funnel of green bushes and grey rocks that zig-zagged between two long low-lying mountains.

His wife took him to the door of their cottage which was itself perched on the spike of a hill; turned him to the necessary direction, and said:

'Follow your nose until you come to Carroll's Pass.'

She slung a crate of fowl on his shoulders and pushed him on the road, calling out:

'Half a crown the chicken and don't bring less, or—!'

He followed his nose.

People passed him, but they passed him the way one goes by a bush or rock, or a cow. He was almost as invisible as these quietudes are, and for the same reason; for who, having seen a cow twice, ever sees a cow again in life? The milkman! Not he, he milks something that he doesn't know is there; but a bull has to be warily met, warily passed, and he bears an uneasy, irresponsible hook beside each

204

of his ears.

One sees a bull perpetually, and one even sees him in places where he is not. But a cow—!

He went down the rough slope; he trudged through the valley and he came to Carroll's Pass.

The world was there before him.

A world of squawks and squeals and grunts and cackles and shrill calls of women and great guffaws of men; with now and then the long lamentable uproar that is made by a donkey pealing above all other noises; and continually, the sharp and gruff and eager bark, yelp, howl, growl, and snarl of every kind of dog that you could put a name to. At a little distance all these noises become one sound and it is as the sound of the sea.

He heard that sound, and he walked into it. It swallowed him up, and therein he disappeared from mortal eye for the space of six hours.

When he reappeared the sun was sinking in a red distance, the fair was all gone home again; there was a deep silence everywhere, and he was as drunk as a lord.

How had he managed it? It is a mystery. He had no longer a crate of chickens on his shoulders. He had no hat. He had no coat. His boots were laced to his feet, so he had them. His trousers were braced to his shoulders and were still his own.

He trod with a kind of cautious happiness into the track of the setting sun, and stood all in a glory of misty gold for a few minutes; then he pointed his nose due west and started for home.

He took two steps to the left, then two steps to the right, then he took one step in front—and then he halted again; readjusted his nose to the compass;

spat on his hands, and had another try at it.

That was his progression, and by balancing his nose on the wind he got forward half a mile in good shape.

He was in the green funnel that wound round between two hills.

Now and then he tried to kick out of his path a rock that was eight feet deep and twenty feet round; now and again he waved a bush from the road with the gesture of one who will be obeyed.

But he was cheerful, he was tolerant, and when these objects refused to budge he went round them and laughed at their discomfiture.

'They,' he said, 'would never think of going round me.'

'Stupid!' said he to a tree, and he dodged it in almost the neatest way imaginable.

Midway in the green and grey funnel there was, for quite a distance on either side, a sudden flattening of the ground. The mountains had, as it were, taken two steps backwards and a narrow mile-long hollow lay between them. The path still ran through this hollow; and here, on either hand, it was bordered by a ditch, into which the hills drained themselves in the wet weather, and which was always moist even in the dry.

He came to this point and undertook the path; but he had the trouble of the world in circumventing the two ditches. They met him everywhere, and instead of being, as they should have been, on his right and left hands, they were continually, unaccountably, in front of him.

But he was cheerful; and each time that he found himself staring into a hole he nodded at it, turned away with a chuckle, balanced his nose on the wind that blew from the west, and won a pace forward.

III

During one of these adjustments, as he stared forward with his chin up, he became aware of the stir of life immediately in front of him; and on this movement he gazed with the gravity of one who understands movement and approves of it.

Two small children were playing on the path. They were prettily dressed, and at a glance one saw that they did not belong to the farmer or labouring class of the neighbourhood. At a distance in front up the hill to the right there was a neat cottage which was sometimes let in the summer months to those folks who have a strange but quickly satisfied liking for country air. There possibly they were at home for a week or two.

The children, a boy and a girl, were very young, perhaps six or seven years of age, and they were playing together. Their game was not in the least complicated. It could be followed by the haziest eye.

They stood each to one side of the road, and then they trotted past each other to the other side of the road. There was a curious, demure deliberation in their play; and there was a curious, demure silence between them.

He looked on these little ones, and his heart filled suddenly with tenderness; he smiled on them from afar, and then, recovering his balance, he moved in their direction.

Every few steps he stood and gazed and wagged

a tender wag at the little ones; and the nearer he drew to them the tenderer he became; but they were intent on their game and did not observe him.

By dint of loving them he became aware that they also loved him; and, when only a small distance away, he lifted his voice in that belief and waved a friendly hand.

The children turned at once in his direction and stood at gaze.

He beckoned to them but they did not move; and the smallest, the most trifling, irritation stirred in his mind. He loved them and they did not run to him! What a singular thing that was. Well, he would go to them; and he at once set about it.

He took two steps to the right. Then he took two steps to the left. Then he took one step forward.

Without a word said, with one sole accord, the two children turned about and trotted down the road.

He was bewildered. He looked at those little legs trotting their demure trot, and it seemed to him that an injustice was being committed. He loved them, and they were running away from him!

He spat on his hands, and took himself to a dog trot after them.

A drunken man walks with great difficulty but he can run with no trouble at all. The quickened action gives him his balance, and the momentum he gets holds him in the balance and in the road. He caught up on the children in two minutes and gripped each of them in a hand that was easily large enough for those small shoulders.

But now he was standing, and his standing was

uneasy. The little girl twisted from his hand and trotted forward again. He shook the little boy with loving violence. The girl trotted back to him, and with all the fury of a tigress but with only the weight of a butterfly, she beat her small fists against his thigh.

'Let out my brother, man,' said she.

He twisted his head round to her, raised his hand, and, with all the irritation of a loving but vexed parent, he slapped her on the cheek. That slap sent the child backwards the width of the road and down into the dust.

He lost his balance, and to save it let go the boy's shoulder. He staggered, waved his arms round and round like the wings of a mill, and, with only half of a balance recaptured, he stared down into a hole.

He went inevitably, almost willingly, into the ditch; and, as he fell, the children, silent still, but with staring eyes, began again their demure little trot down the road.

He nodded gravely at the bottom of the ditch and he spoke gravely to it.

'I'll teach you,' said he, 'to run away from me.'

Then he placed his cheek carefully on a large soft piece of mud and went peacefully to sleep.

A Rhinoceros, Some Ladies
and A Horse

One day, in my first job, a lady fell in love with me.
It was quite unreasonable, of course, for I wasn't
wonderful: I was small and thin, and I weighed
much the same as a largish duck-egg. I didn't fall in
love with her, or anything like that. I got under the
table, and stayed there until she had to go wherever
she had to go to.

I had seen an advertisement—'Smart boy wanted',
it said. My legs were the smartest things about me,
so I went there on the run. I got the job.

At that time there was nothing on God's earth
that I could do, except run. I had no brains, and I
had no memory. When I was told to do anything I
got into such an enthusiasm about it that I couldn't
remember anything else about it. I just ran as hard
as I could, and then I ran back, proud and panting.
And when they asked me for the whatever-it-was
that I had run for, I started, right on the instant, and
ran some more.

The place I was working at was, amongst other
things, a theatrical agency. I used to be sitting in a

corner of the office floor, waiting to be told to run somewhere and back. A lady would come in—a music-hall lady that is—and, in about five minutes, howls of joy would start coming from the inner office. Then, peacefully enough, the lady and my two bosses would come out, and the lady always said, 'Splits! I can do splits like no one.' And one of my bosses would say, 'I'm keeping your splits in mind.' And the other would add, gallantly—'No one who ever saw your splits could ever forget 'em.'

One of my bosses was thin, and the other one was fat. My fat boss was composed entirely of stomachs. He had three baby-stomachs under his chin: then he had three more descending in even larger englobings nearly to the ground: but, just before reaching the ground, the final stomach bifurcated into a pair of boots. He was very light on these and could bounce about in the neatest way.

He was the fattest thing I had ever seen, except a rhinoceros that I had met in the Zoo the Sunday before I got the job. That rhino was *very* fat, and it had a smell like twenty-five pigs. I was standing outside its palisade, wondering what it could possibly feel like to be a rhinoceros, when two larger boys passed by. Suddenly they caught hold of me, and pushed me through the bars of the palisade. I was very skinny, and in about two seconds I was right inside, and the rhinoceros was looking at me.

It was very fat, but it wasn't fat like stomachs, it was fat like barrels of cement, and when it moved it creaked a lot, like a woman I used to know who creaked like an old bedstead. The rhinoceros swaggled over to me with a bunch of cabbage sticking out of its mouth. It wasn't angry, or anything like that, it just wanted to see who I was. Rhinos are blindish: they mainly see by smelling, and they smell in snorts. This one started at my left shoe, and snorted right up that side of me to my ear. He smelt that very carefully: then he switched over to my right ear, and snorted right down that side of me to my right shoe: then he fell in love with my shoes and began to lick them. I, naturally, wriggled my feet at that, and the big chap was so astonished that he did the strangest step-dance backwards to his pile of cabbages, and began to eat them.

I squeezed myself out of his cage and walked away. In a couple of minutes I saw the two boys. They were very frightened, and they asked me what I had done to the rhinoceros. I answered, a bit grandly, perhaps, that I had seized it in both hands, ripped it limb from limb, and tossed its carcase to the crows. But when they began shouting to people that I had just murdered a rhinoceros I took to my heels, for I didn't want to be arrested and hanged for a murder that I hadn't committed.

Still, a man can't be as fat as a rhinoceros, but my boss was as fat as a man can be. One day a great lady of the halls came in, and was received on the knee. She was very great. Her name was Maudie Darling, or thereabouts. My bosses called her nothing but 'Darling,' and she called them the same. When the time came for her to arrive the whole building got palpitations of the heart. After waiting a while my thin boss got angry, and said—'Who does the woman think she is? If she isn't here in two twos I'll go down to the entry, and when she does come I'll boot her out.' The fat boss said—'She's only two hours late, she'll be here before the week's out.'

Within a few minutes there came great clamours from the courtyard. Patriotic cheers, such as Parnell himself never got, were thundering. My bosses ran instantly to the inner office. Then the door opened, and the lady appeared.

She was very wide, and deep, and magnificent. She was dressed in camels and zebras and goats: she had two peacocks in her hat and a rabbit muff in her hand, and she strode among these with prancings.

But when she got right into the room and saw herself being looked at by three men and a boy she became adorably shy: one could see that she had never been looked at before.

'O,' said she, with a smile that made three and a half hearts beat like one, 'O,' said she, very modestly, 'is Mr. Which-of-'em-is-it really in? Please tell him that Little-Miss-Me would be so glad to see and to be—'

Then the inner door opened, and the large lady was surrounded by my fat boss and my thin boss. She crooned to them—'O, you dear boys, you'll never know how much I've thought of you and longed to see you.'

That remark left me stupefied. The first day I got to the office I heard that it was the fat boss's birthday, and that he was thirty years of age: and the thin boss didn't look a day younger than the fat one. How the lady could mistake these old men for boys seemed to me the strangest fact that had ever come my way. My own bet was that they'd both die of old age in about a month.

After a while they all came out again. The lady

was helpless with laughter: she had to be supported by my two bosses—'O,' she cried, 'you boys will kill me.' And the bosses laughed and laughed, and the fat one said—'Darling, you're a scream,' and the thin one said—'Darling, you're a riot.'

And then . . . she saw me! I saw her seeing me the very way I had seen the rhinoceros seeing me: I wondered for an instant would she smell me down one leg and up the other. She swept my two bosses right away from her, and she became a kind of queen, very glorious to behold: but sad, startled. She stretched a long, slow arm out and out and and then she unfolded a long, slow finger, and pointed it at me—'Who is THAT??' she whispered in a strange whisper that could be heard two miles off.

My fat boss was an awful liar—'The cat brought that in,' said he.

But the thin boss rebuked him: 'No,' he said, 'it was not the cat. Let me introduce you; darling, this is James. James, this is the darling of the gods.'

'And of the pit,' said she, sternly.

She looked at me again. Then she sank to her knees and spread out both arms to me—

'Come to my boozalum, angel,' said she in a tender kind of way.

I knew what she meant, and I knew that she didn't know how to pronounce that word. I took a rapid glance at the area indicated. The lady had a boozalum you could graze a cow on. I didn't wait one second, but slid, in one swift, silent slide, under the table. Then she came forward and said a whole lot of poems to me under the table, imploring me, among a lot of odd things, to 'come forth, and gild

214

the morning with my eyes,' but at last she was reduced to whistling at me with two fingers in her
mouth, the way you whistle for a cab.

I learned after she had gone that most of the
things she said to me were written by a poet fellow
named Spokeshave. They were very complimentary,
but I couldn't love a woman who mistook my old
bosses for boys, and had a boozalum that it would
take an Arab chieftain a week to trot across on a
camel.

The thin boss pulled me from under the table by
my leg, and said that my way was the proper way
to treat a rip, but my fat boss said, very gravely—
'James, when a lady invites a gentleman to her
boozalum a real gentleman hops there as pronto as
possible, and I'll have none but real gentlemen in
this office.'

'Tell me,' he went on, 'what made that wad of
Turkish Delight fall in love with you?'

'She didn't love me at all, sir,' I answered.

'No?' he inquired.

'She was making fun of me,' I explained.

'There's something in that,' said he seriously,
and went back to his office.

I had been expecting to be sacked that day. I was
sacked the next day, but that was about a horse.

I had been given three letters to post, and told to
run or they'd be too late. So I ran to the post office
and round it and back, with, naturally, the three
letters in my pocket. As I came to our door a nice,
solid, red-faced man rode up on a horse. He thrust
the reins into my hand—

'Hold the horse for a minute,' said he.

'I can't,' I replied, 'my boss is waiting for me.'

'I'll only be a minute,' said he angrily, and he walked off.

Well, there was I, saddled, as it were, with a horse. I looked at it, and it looked at me. Then it blew a pint of soap-suds out of its nose and took another look at me, and then the horse fell in love with me as if he had just found his long-lost foal. He started to lean against me and to woo me with small whinneys, and I responded and replied as best I could.

'Don't move a toe,' said I to the horse, 'I'll be back in a minute.'

He understood exactly what I said, and the only move he made was to swing his head and watch me as I darted up the street. I was less than half a minute away anyhow, and never out of his sight.

Up the street there was a man, and sometimes a woman, with a barrow, thick-piled with cabbages and oranges and apples. As I raced round the barrow I pinched an apple off it at full speed, and in ten seconds I was back at the horse. The good nag had watched every move I made, and when I got back his eyes were wide open, his mouth was wide open, and he had his legs all splayed out so that he couldn't possibly slip. I broke the apple in halves and popped one half into his mouth. He ate it in slow crunches, and then he looked diligently at the other half. I gave him the other half, and, as he ate it, he gurgled with cidery gargles of pure joy. He then swung his head round from me and pointed his nose up the street, right at the apple-barrow.

I raced up the street again, and was back within the half-minute with another apple. The horse had nigh finished the first half of it when a man who had come up said, thoughtfully—

216

'He seems to like apples, bedad!'

'He loves them,' said I.

And then, exactly at the speed of lightning, the man became angry, and invented bristles all over himself like a porcupine.

'What the hell do you mean,' he hissed, and then he bawled, 'by stealing my apples?'

I retreated a bit into the horse.

'I didn't steal your apples,' I said.

'You didn't!' he roared, and then he hissed, 'I saw you,' he hissed.

'I didn't steal them,' I explained, 'I pinched them.'

'Tell me that one again,' said he.

'If,' said I patiently, 'if I took the apples for myself that would be stealing.'

'So it would,' he agreed.

'But as I took them for the horse that's pinching.'

'Be dam, but!' said he. ''Tis a real argument,' he went on, staring at the sky. 'Answer me that one,' he demanded of himself, and he is a very stupor of intellection. 'I give it up,' he roared, 'you give me back my apples.'

I placed the half apple that was left into his hand, and he looked at it as if it was a dead frog.

'What'll I do with that?' he asked earnestly.

'Give it to the horse,' said I.

The horse was now prancing at him, and mincing at him, and making love at him. He pushed the half apple into the horse's mouth, and the horse mumbled it and watched him, and chewed it and watched him, and gurgled it and watched him.

'He does like his bit of apple,' said the man.

'He likes you too,' said I. 'I think he loves you.

'It looks like it,' he agreed, for the horse was

yearning at him, and its eyes were soulful.

'Let's get him another apple,' said I, and, without another word, we both pounded back to his barrow and each of us pinched an apple off it. We got one apple into the horse, and were breaking the second one when a woman said gently—

'Nice, kind, Christian gentlemen, feeding dumb animals—with my apples,' she yelled suddenly.

The man with me jumped as if he had been hit by a train.

'Mary,' said he humbly.

'Joseph,' said she in a completely unloving voice.

But the woman transformed herself into nothing else but woman—

'What about my apples?' said she. 'How many have we lost?'

'Three,' said Joseph.

'Four,' said I, 'I pinched three and you pinched one.'

'That's true,' said he. 'That's exact, Mary. I only pinched one of our apples.'

'You only,' she squealed.

And I, hoping to be useful, broke in—

'Joseph,' said I, 'is the nice lady your boss?'

He halted for a dreadful second, and made up his mind.

'You bet she's my boss,' said he, 'and she's better than that, for she's the very wife of my bosum.'

She turned to me.

'Child of Grace—' said she—

Now, when I was a child, and did something that a woman didn't like she always expostulated in the same way. If I tramped on her foot, or jabbed her in the stomach—the way women have mulitudes of feet and stomachs is always astonishing to a child—the remark such a woman made was always the same. She would grab her toe or her stomach, and say—'Childagrace, what the hell are you doing?' After a while I worked it out that Childagrace was one word, and was my name. When any woman in agony yelled Childagrace I ran right up prepared to be punished, and the woman always said tenderly, 'What are you yowling about, Childagrace.'

'Childagrace,' said Mary earnestly, 'how's my family to live if you steal our apples? You take my livelihood away from me! Very good, but will you feed and clothe and educate my children in,' she continued proudly, 'the condition to which they are accustomed?'

I answered that question cautiously.

'How many kids have you, ma'am?' said I.

'We'll leave that alone for a while,' she went on. 'You owe me two and six for the apples.'

'Mary!' said Joseph, in a pained voice.

'And you,' she snarled at him, 'owe me three shillings. I'll take it out of you in pints.' She turned to me.

'What do you do with all the money you get from the office here?'

'I give it to my landlady.'

'Does she stick to the lot of it?'

'Oh, no,' I answered, 'she always gives me back threepence.'

'Well, you come and live with me and I'll give you back fourpence.'

'All right,' said I.

'By gum,' said Joseph, enthusiastically, 'that'll be fine. We'll go out every night and we won't steal a thing. We'll just pinch legs of beef, and pig's feet, and barrels of beer—'

'Wait now,' said Mary. 'You stick to your own landlady. I've trouble enough of my own. You needn't pay me the two and six.'

'Good for you,' said Joseph heartily, and then, to me—

'You just get a wife of your bosum half as kind as my wife of my bosum and you'll be set up for life. 'Mary,' he cried joyfully, 'let's go and have a pint on the strength of it.'

'You shut up,' said she.

'Joseph,' I interrupted, 'knows how to pronounce the word properly.'

'What word?'

'The one he used when he said you were the wife of his what-you-may-call-it.'

'I'm not the wife of any man's what-you-may-call-it,' said she, indignantly—'Oh, I see what you mean! So he pronounced it well, did he?'

'Yes, ma'am.'

She looked at me very sternly—

'How does it come you know about all these kinds of words?'

'Yes,' said Joseph, and he was even sterner than she was, 'when I was your age I didn't know any bad words.'

'You shut up,' said she, and continued, 'what made you say that to me?'

'A woman came into our office yesterday, and she mispronounced it.'

'What did she say now?'

'Oh, she said it all wrong.'

'Do you tell me so? We're all friends here: what

220

way did she say it, son?'

'Well, ma'am, she called it boozalum.'

'She said it wrong all right,' said Joseph, 'but 'tis a good, round, fat kind of a word all the same.'

'You shut up,' said Mary. 'Who did she say the word to?'

'She said it to me, ma'am.'

'She must have been a rip,' said Joseph.

'Was she a rip, now?'

'I don't know, ma'am. I never met a rip.'

'You're too young yet,' said Joseph, 'but you'll meet them later on. I never met a rip myself until I got married—I mean,' he added hastily, 'that they were all rips except the wife of my what-do-you-call-ems, and that's why I married her.'

'I expect you've got a barrel-full of rips in your past,' said she bleakly, 'you must tell me about some of them tonight.' And then, to me, 'tell us about the woman,' said she.

So I told them all about her, and how she held out her arms to me, and said, 'Come to my boozalum, angel.'

'What did you do when she shoved out the old arms at you?' said Joseph.

'I got under the table,' I answered.

'That's not a bad place at all, but,' he continued earnestly, 'never get under the bed when there's an old girl chasing you, for that's the worst spot you could pick on. What was the strap's name?'

'Maudie Darling, she called herself.'

'You're a blooming lunatic,' said Joseph, 'she's the loveliest thing in the world, barring,' he added hastily, 'the wife of my blast-the-bloody-word.'

'We saw her last night,' said Mary, 'at Dan Lowrey's Theatre, and she's just lovely.'

'She isn't as nice as you, ma'am,' I asserted.

'Do you tell me that now?' said she.

'You are twice as nice as she is, and twenty times nicer.'

'There you are,' said Joseph, 'the very words I said to you last night.'

'You shut up,' said Mary scornfully, 'you were trying to knock a pint out of me! Listen, son,' she went on, 'we'll take all that back about your land-lady. You come and live with me, and I'll give you back sixpence a week out of your wages.'

'All right, ma'am,' I crowed in a perfectly mon-strous joy.

'Mary,' said Joseph, in a reluctant voice—

'You shut up,' said she.

'He can't come to live with us,' said Joseph. 'He's a bloody Prodestan,' he added sadly.

'Why—' she began—

'He'd keep me and the childer up all night, pinch-ing apples for horses and asses, and reading the Bible, and up to every kind of devilment.'

Mary made up her mind quickly.

'You stick to your own landlady,' said she, 'tell her that I said she was to give you sixpence.' She whirled about. 'There won't be a thing left on that barrow,' said she to Joseph.

'Damn the scrap,' said Joseph violently.

'Listen,' said Mary to me very earnestly, 'am I nicer than Maudie Darling?'

'You are ma'am,' said I.

Mary went down on the road on her knees: she stretched out both arms to me, and said—

'Come to my boozalum, angel.'

222

I looked at her, and I looked at Joseph, and I looked at the horse. Then I turned from them all and ran into the building and into the office. My fat boss met me—

'Here's your five bob,' said he. 'Get to hell out of here,' said he.

And I ran out.

I went to the horse, and leaned my head against the thick end of his neck, and the horse leaned as much of himself against me as he could manage. Then the man who owned the horse came up and climbed into his saddle. He fumbled in his pocket—

'You were too long,' said I. 'I've been sacked for minding your horse.'

'That's too bad,' said he: 'that's too damn bad,' and he tossed me a penny.

I caught it, and lobbed it back into his lap, and I strode down the street the most outraged human being then living in the world.